THE LEGEND

of

LILIA

CHRISTOPHER P. REDWINE

A NOVEL
BASED ON A
TRUE STORY

"Whoever does not miss the Soviet Union
has no heart. Whoever wants it back has no brain."
—Vladimir Putin

Chapter 1

On a warm day in the summer of 1936, Lilia Vladimirovna Litvyak sat in the cockpit of a Polykarpov PO-2 biplane, staring down the runway alone. The tips of her blonde hair showed under the edges of her flight cap, her blue grey eyes covered in goggles.

"Are you ready, Lilia?" said the flight instructor, ready to crank the propeller.

"I'm ready," she replied.

"You'll have only yourself to rely on," he followed.

"Start it up!" she answered back.

The flight instructor leaned in hard, cranking over the wooden propeller, and with a thump and a sputter the wood and canvas machine came to life. The propeller spun into a blur and the engine sent rumbles through the airframe. The flight instructor stepped aside as she pushed the throttle forward. The biplane rolled down the runway, quickly gaining speed. The nose dipped as the back wheel lifted up. A little more speed and the biplane lifted off the runway, climbing into the sky. People on the ground grew smaller and smaller. Soon the buildings of Moscow would come into view. She flew above roads and houses and onion domed churches. A farmer stood in a field below, beside his horse and cart, waving to her. For the first time in her life, she was alone amongst the clouds.

As a child, she had been fascinated for as long as she could remember that it was possible for people to fly. Pointing to the sky at each rare sighting of an airplane, it became the singular goal of her young life to know how it felt to be up in the clouds looking down on the world. By age fifteen, Lilia had joined the Kalinin Air Club outside of Moscow. She had completed her ground school training, learning in a classroom the mechanics of how an airplane interacted with the air around it, and how to control it with throttle, pedals, and stick, and how to read the cockpit gauges and why they were each important. After passing her tests in the classroom, she flew with an instructor who would take off and land the plane but gave her the controls once in the air. She learned quickly how to pull the airplane through turns, and to climb and descend.

For Lilia, the summer of 1936 passed idyllically. She filled her days with frequent flights from the Kalinin airfield and bus rides home to her family's apartment in Moscow. She would return in the evenings to find her mother cooking supper, while her father read the paper, and her younger brother Yuri, just six years old, colored in books or played with toys. Her father Vladimir and mother Anna had moved to Moscow from the country after the revolution, trading a life of farming for a life in the city. Vladimir had found training as a railroad engineer and worked hard to make his way up the ranks to become a Minister in the Department of Transportation. Lilia's mother Anna worked by day as a seamstress.

While flying, Lilia focused her thoughts on the airplane, getting to know its feel a little more with each flight, giving little thought to any problems on the ground. But with each passing day, the people she encountered seemed to change. Their eyes were cast down as they walked the streets of Moscow, ever more distrustful of one another. In August of that year, Lilia's father would read in the newspaper the details of Stalin's show trials. His political opponents had been put on trial, accused of treason against the Soviet state. On every street corner one could sense a darkening mood amongst the people, and in hushed voices passed the stories of people disappearing in the night. There were even whispered rumors that the security apparatus was always listening with hidden microphones, desperate to know what the people said to each other when they believed they were alone.

Lilia's father, Vladimir, didn't share this darkened mood. She had always known him to be an optimist, encouraging her at every chance to believe in herself and never to give up when facing a difficult task. He had gotten himself from a rural life on a farm to a job in Moscow with hard work and optimism and the firmly held belief that life for the average Russian was improving. The conveniences of the modern world; radio, telephones, electricity, and mass transportation were just coming into reach for all. A new era of modern life was about to be born. Lilia followed his attitude on the world and by the age of fifteen it had earned her a pilot's license.

The summer passed and the fall arrived. Lilia returned to school and took flights from the airfield on weekends. The leaves turned from green to red and gold, then fell from the trees. The nights grew colder and the streets became quieter. The rumors that passed in hushed voices persisted, and a vague sense of fear was never far. On a cold night in October, three shiny black sedans came to a stop outside the Litvyaks' apartment building. Four officers of the People's Commissariat for Internal Affairs, the NKVD, stepped out in green uniforms with blue caps, holding black nightsticks, pistols holstered on their belts. The black sedans would be heard driving the streets of Moscow late at night when everyone was asleep, or lying awake in fear that tonight the Black Ravens, as they were called, might come for them.

Lilia, her mother Anna, father Vladimir, and her brother Yuri were all asleep, even at the thumping of boots climbing the stairs to their apartment. Lilia woke to the sound of a hard clacking on the front door, and a shout to "Open up!"

Lilia jumped quickly out of bed and looked at the clock. It was just after 4 AM. What could this be? She stepped out of her bedroom to find her mother Anna staring at the front door, frozen in fear. Her father followed behind her wrapping himself in a robe as the clacking of the nightstick repeated.

"Open up!" the voice shouted again.

"Who is it?" Vladimir replied. If he was afraid, it didn't show.

Anna pleaded to her husband in a hushed voice, "Don't open the door."

"Vladimir Litvyak, we must speak with you. Open this door."

Anna shook her head, pleading with him not to open it. Perhaps they would give up and go away. Lilia watched in silence. She turned to see Yuri appear at the door to his room.

"Yuri, go back to sleep," she said, pushing him back.

"What's happening?" he asked.

"Stay in your room, and go back to sleep," Lilia said again, trying to keep calm. She closed the door to his room softly.

Vladimir stared at the front door, thinking to himself that there must be a mistake. He had worked hard in his job, and kept his political opinions to himself, never speaking ill of the Communist Party or of Stalin. What could they want with him? He nudged his wife Anna aside and undid the latch. Three NKVD Officers stood in the doorway.

"What is the great emergency at this hour?" he asked of them.

"Vladimir Litvyak, we have a warrant for your arrest. You're coming with us," said an officer, walking through the doorway with the other two to take Vladimir by the arms.

"No. This must be a mistake. He's done nothing wrong. He's committed no crime," Anna pleaded.

As Lilia watched her father being taken from the apartment, she could hear the rapping of nightsticks on the doors of her neighbors. "Come out!" the voices shouted.

The barking of a neighbor's small dog down the hall was followed by a gunshot, and the animal's dying whimper.

Anna followed the officers as they took Vladimir down the stairs by his elbows, urging them to stop. Lilia followed after her mother. By the time they reached the street below, it seemed the entire neighborhood had been woken from sleep and brought outside. Vladimir was quickly shoved into the back seat of a black sedan. He looked out to Anna and Lilia, helpless. Anna, now in tears, was pushed away from the car as more NKVD Officers emerged from the apartment building across the street. Holding another man by his elbows, the officers ushered him into the back seat next to Vladimir and the doors were shut. Lilia felt the salty sting of tears on her face. She looked to the faces of her neighbors, some she had known her whole life. Their eyes were cast down in shame, avoiding her glance.

Three more NKVD Officers emerged from the building across the street carrying armfuls of books and dropped them in a pile in the middle of Novoslobodskaya Street.

Another NKVD Officer stood on the running boards of one of the black sedans. "We have rooted out terrorists, right here in this very neighborhood," the officer shouted. "They are charged with crimes of subversion and possession of illegal literature. Thankfully, one of you has informed us of these dangerous activities." He addressed the crowd while another officer poured gasoline on the pile of books. "They are enemies of the people," he continued. "There is no place in our society for class enemies! Nothing will stop our new Soviet nation from moving forward, to progress!" He roared to his silent audience as a match was thrown on the pile of books, sending up orange flames. He climbed down from the running board and got into the car.

Vladimir Litvyak stared out the back window as the Black Ravens sped away. Anna and her daughter, tears in their eyes, looked to the faces of their neighbors. They avoided her gaze, shuffling back to their apartments by the orange light of books burning in the street. What would come to be known as 'The Great Terror' had begun. For the next two years the Black Ravens would make their rounds in the night, arresting more than a million people, many of whose fate was execution, or a long sentence of hard labor only to die in the gulags of Siberia. The people lived in a state of fear, of the late night rapping of a nightstick on a door, and silent relief when the black ravens had not come for them, but their neighbor instead. Someone else would be amongst the disappeared, their name no longer to be spoken.

A week later, on a cold day in autumn, Anna Litvyak huddled against the long grey wall of the Lubyanka prison. She stood in line with hundreds of other women, all waiting to learn the fate of husbands, fathers, and sons, disappeared in the night. Snow flurries blew across the square, past the line of women that wrapped around the building. Most kept silent, but Anna had struck up a conversation with the young woman in front of her. She had grown up on a farm, like Anna, where she met the man she would marry. He was several years her senior and a tailor by trade. He had courted the young woman and won the permission of her parents. He had brought her from a life in the country of hard work, to a life of relative ease in Moscow.

It was at the end of a long day of cutting and sewing that her husband had set aside his needle, and so as not to lose it, stuck it in a newspaper by his side. He hadn't noticed that the needle was stuck into a photograph of a Communist Party official, squarely in the eye. One of his customers had noticed and informed the NKVD. The rapping at their door came unexpectedly, just after 4 A.M. as well. None of her neighbors had dared to open their doors to see what the commotion was about. They kept silent in their own apartments, relieved it wasn't happening to them.

The long line moved slowly as the young woman told Anna her story, moving ever closer to an NKVD officer seated at a table set up outside the front door of the prison. As each woman offered a name, he would search through large bound ledgers to find the name of the accused and read the results of their trial and sentencing. None were found innocent. Anna had watched for the better part of the morning as one by one another woman would be told the sentence and walk away in tears. Soon it would be her turn to learn the fate of her husband, Vladimir. The young woman in front of Anna stepped up to the table and spoke the name of her husband, then waited breathlessly as the officer flipped through the ledgers to discover his fate.

"Your husband was found guilty, and was sentenced to ten years labor," he said without emotion. She stood before him confused, somehow waiting for more. Tears welled in her eyes as she stared at the officer. "Don't cry. There is hope you will see him again one day," he finally offered. The young woman sank, turned and walked away as all of those before her had done.

The officer turned his glance to Anna and waited. Anna stepped forward nervously and spoke only two words *"Vladimir Litvyak."* An eternity passed as the officer again flipped through the ledgers, enough time for Anna to notice the snow flurries blowing across the square and look back at the long grey line of women behind her. The officer's finger stopped on one line in the middle of the thick book.

The NKVD officer looked up to Anna coldly and said "Vladimir Litvyak was convicted of his crime and sentenced to execution. The sentence has been carried out."

Anna had tried to prepare herself for the worst but couldn't allow herself to believe this could be it. She stared at the officer in disbelief, who simply waited for Anna to accept the news and walk away like so many others.

"He did nothing wrong," Anna said, waiting for an answer.

"Our faith in the party and in our Soviet nation must be pure. We must all sacrifice for the purity of our motherland in some way," the officer replied. "Consider this to have been yours."

It was hopeless. Anna's husband was gone, murdered by the state security apparatus. She looked at the long line of women behind her again. There were only cold stares, no offers of kindness. Anna turned and walked away, trying to hide her tears.

Lilia returned to the family's apartment in the evening to find Anna and her brother Yuri huddled together in the living room. Their eyes were red from several hours of crying. Lilia knew immediately the news would be bad and stared at her mother to wait for it.

"He's gone," Anna said.

"Gone?" Lilia replied. "What do you mean, gone?"

"He's been executed," Anna said calmly.

Lilia put her hands on her stomach as a rush of pain suddenly burned inside of her with such intensity she could hardly breath. Anna held her daughter in her arms as she cried, but it was the end of childhood innocence. It occurred to Lilia that everything one could ever have would inevitably be lost. Her next thought provoked only a feeling of helplessness - 'What now?' How would they continue on with their lives?

Lilia lay in bed that night, trying to sleep, while the uncertainty of the future kept her awake. What would she say when anyone asked of her father? That he had simply disappeared like so many others? Would they come back for Anna, or for her? By morning, a feeling of confusion and maddening frustration had wrapped itself around her, constricting her with each new thought until she could hold only one. She must get back in the air.

At first light, Lilia rushed out of the family apartment. The city was still asleep when she caught a bus to the Kalinin airfield, an hour ride north of Moscow. The Airclub Commander had already fueled a blue biplane and given it a pre-flight check. He noticed the intensity on her face.

"Are you feeling well today, Lilia?" he asked before signing her into the ledger.

"Anxious to get back in the air," she responded.

With a nod, he signed the form, then unblocked the wheels and pushed the flying machine out of the hangar and positioned it on the runway. Lilia strapped on her flying helmet and goggles and climbed into the cockpit. She strapped herself in tight as the Airclub Commander steadied his grip on the propeller. Lilia stared down the runway once more.

"Are you ready, Lilia?" he asked.

"Start it up," she declared.

He threw the propeller into motion and stepped away as the airplane came to life. Lilia pushed the throttle forward. The biplane rolled ahead, picking up speed. The nose dipped and the biplane lifted off the runway and climbed into the sky.

Absent were the bright blue sky and the tall white clouds of summer. The sky over Moscow was a cold grey in the distance. Lilia pushed the airplane through a gentle turn, alone in the sky with her thoughts. As the memories of her father entered her mind, she kicked hard on the pedals, throwing the biplane into a barrel roll. The horizon spun into view as she flipped the airplane upside down and back again. She leveled it off then pushed the stick forward full throttle, the airplane picking up speed. She pulled hard on the stick and held it back. The biplane climbed into a full loop, the engine buzzing as hard as it could pull.

Lilia threw the airplane into a series of twists and rolls, thrashing the biplane around in the sky. She pushed the airplane to its limit, a wooden propeller, mounted to a metal engine, mounted to wood and canvas and wire. How much could it take before something snapped? She pulled back on the stick again, at full throttle until the airplane nosed straight up and away from the Earth. The airplane climbed until the pressure of her back against the seat gave way. The biplane hung in the air motionless, and for a moment she was weightless.

The biplane nosed down again. Gaining speed, the ground below came into view in a dizzying spiral, earth fast approaching. If she held down the stick or did nothing it could all be over. The pain, anger, and frustration could be cured in an instant. The airplane of wood and canvas would be smashed to bits and herself along with it. As the ground rushed at her quickly, the biplane spiraling to certain death, she thought again of her father, Vladimir.

Lilia kicked the pedals and pulled back on the stick, correcting the airplane out its spiral, pushed the throttle forward and held the stick back, leveling off two meters from the ground before climbing again. It was not the time to quit. Her life and her destiny were still her own to choose and they would not be taken without a fight. "Be strong." she told herself. "Never give up on your life. He wouldn't want it."

Chapter 2

In June of 1941, Adolph Hitler launched Operation Barbarossa. The German Army had smashed through the Soviet border with tanks and artillery and almost four million troops. The Luftwaffe was equally effective, quickly claiming air superiority, destroying over two thousand Soviet airplanes on the first day. In the months to follow, the German Army tore a path of destruction across the Eastern Front in tank battles and ground warfare, right to the edge of Moscow.

With the Soviet air force in disarray, Joseph Stalin authorized the formation of three air combat regiments to be comprised exclusively of female pilots. The three regiments were to be led by Marina Raskova, the most famous female aviator of the Soviet Union, and the first woman to become a navigator in the Soviet Air Force. She had set an aviation record for the longest flight, with two other women, Polina Osipenko and Valentina Grizodubova. When their aircraft had become burdened with ice, Marina Raskova was first to parachute from the airplane before a crash landing and was lost and separated from the others for ten days without food or water. All survived and for this record flight, all three became the first women to ever be awarded their nation's highest honor, the Gold Star for Hero of the Soviet Union.

At the start of the war, Lilia was recruited to train male pilots for the front, and the Kalinin Air Club was converted to a military facility. By October of 1941, Lilia had trained forty-five pilots in all. The young men were given only twenty hours of flight training, and then sent to almost certain death against the far more experienced pilots of Hitler's Luftwaffe. The German Army had gotten close enough to send flights over Moscow. Riding the bus back and forth to the airfield, Lilia would pass the rubble of destroyed buildings scattered throughout Moscow, and occasionally look up to see Luftwaffe planes. As a child, she would be excited to spot an airplane, but now they were enemy planes bombing her city. She could shoot them down if only they would give her the chance, she thought. When news of the formation of female air regiments reached the airfield, Lilia knew she would get that chance.

Recruitment for the women's air regiments took place at the Zhukovsky Academy in Moscow, with Marina Raskova conducting personal interviews with each applicant. Lilia hopped off a bus in front of the Zhukovsky Academy. Once a Tsarist palace, a red star adorned the gate. Sandbag pillboxes and anti-aircraft guns had replaced the palace's once elegant garden. Lilia passed through the gates and up the stairs to find a Corporal sitting at a desk by the entrance.

"I've come to sign up for the Women's Air Regiment," she said.

"Down the hallway and take the stairs to the second floor," he replied.

On the second floor, Lilia found the long, high-ceilinged corridor filled with Russian girls waiting on benches along the sides of the hallway. They chatted excitedly amongst themselves. Lilia walked confidently past them toward a clerk seated at a desk at the end of the hall. Eighteen-year old Fayina Pleshivtseva, sandy-haired, an overcoat wrapped tightly around her slender figure, sat on a bench watching Lilia. "How could this little girl ever become a soldier?" she thought to herself. Lilia looked out of place, shorter than the others, still in her flight jacket and coveralls, a satchel over her shoulder, while the others wore dresses and overcoats.

"I'm here to sign up for the fighter regiment," Lilia told the clerk.

"Sign the list. We'll call when it's your turn," he said, pushing a clipboard toward her.

Lilia signed her name and looked for an empty seat. Not finding one, she leaned against a wall next to Fayina, who continued watching her curiously. Lilia turned to meet her gaze.

"You a pilot too?" Lilia asked.

"Yes." Fayina replied.

"For what regiment are you going to be flying?" Lilia probed.

"Doesn't look like I'll be flying in any regiment." Fayina offered. "Not enough hours in the air. They want me to be a mechanic."

"How many hours have you got?" Lilia wondered.

"Four-hundred-thirty-eight." Fayina sighed.

"And they won't let you fly? That's ridiculous," Lilia said.

"The men train for twenty hours before they send them up. For us, it's five hundred, and that's just for night bombers. It's eight hundred for day bombers, and a thousand for fighters," Fayina replied. "I would have been a great fighter pilot," she added.

"One thousand hours..." Lilia spoke slowly, thinking to herself. "Excuse me." Lilia turned and walked down the hall. She ducked into an adjacent hallway to stop at a nook in a windowsill halfway up another flight of stairs. She didn't have a thousand hours flight time and she knew it. Sitting in the windowsill, she took her flight log out of the satchel and studied it. She reached into the satchel and found a pen. Studying the log entries, she quickly wrote over the numbers. Her pen stopped on a "1". She wrote over it, changing it to a "2." A "6" became an "8" further down the page. Quickly and methodically, she had added more than one hundred hours to the total. Lilia returned to the hall just as the clerk called out her name.

"Wish me luck," she said to Fayina as she walked past.

"Flight log, please" said the clerk.

Lilia handed over her flight log, waiting nervously as he opened it and began to add up the hours. Below the last entry he drew a line and wrote the total, '1,012 hours,' and put his initials next to it. Lilia smiled as he handed it back and motioned her toward an office behind him.

Behind a large wooden desk sat the legendary Marina Raskova, straight dark hair, and a stern face. Lilia felt a pinch of nervousness as she walked into the office to stand before her. Lilia had read all about her famous flights and of her Gold Star as a Hero of the Soviet Union.

"Please, sit," said Marina Raskova.

Lilia sat down, still holding her flight log, ready to present it.

"Your flight log?" Marina asked.

Lilia handed the logbook across the large desk and waited as Marina studied it, finding the total of 1,012 hours.

"It seems you have quite a lot of hours in the air for a girl your age," Major Raskova finally offered.

"I got my pilot's license at fifteen. I've been training pilots for the front for the last five months," Lilia said, "forty-five in all."

"And now you want to fly at the front yourself?" Marina asked in a serious voice.

"In fighter planes," Lilia said decisively.

"You do understand that flying at the front will be nothing like the air clubs?" Marina said.

"I understand the risk," Lilia replied.

"You could be killed or injured. You could see friends killed and injured," Marina continued. "You might be injured so badly your own mother wouldn't recognize you. And you still wish to join?"

Lilia paused a moment, then answered, "Very much."

Marina Raskova stood, and held out her hand. "Welcome to the regiment," she said with a smile.

Lilia rode a bus straight home, then started to pack. What would she need? How does one pack for a war? She was expected at the Moscow central train station with all the other recruits that had been accepted the next morning. As she contemplated what to bring, she saw her mother standing in the doorway.

"I've joined the Women's Air Regiment," Lilia told her. "I'm going to the front to fight."

"You could be killed, Lilia." Anna said.

"I could be killed if I stay here," Lily replied. "The Germans are close enough to send planes to drop bombs on us. I could shoot them down."

Anna knew there was nothing that would change Lilia's mind.

"When do you leave?" Anna asked.

"Tomorrow morning," Lilia said calmly.

"What about your father?" Anna asked.

"They're desperate for pilots, and I'm a good one. Perhaps that's more important," Lilia replied. "They can't call us enemies of the people when the war is over and I've saved their country? I'll be fighting for us all. Then what will people say about the name Litvyak?"

"I don't want to lose my daughter too," said Anna.

"I will return to you, Mamushka, I promise." Lilia replied, embracing her mother.

The next morning, Lilia arrived at the Moscow central train station to find her fellow recruits searching through piles of military uniforms, pants, shirts, and boots. The uniforms had all been intended for men. The best fitting ones were still many sizes too large. The sleeves of Lilia's uniform hung well past her hands, and her baggy pant legs had to be rolled up so she wouldn't trip on them. Fayina spotted her and began to laugh.

"Just picture the men who got our uniforms," Lilia responded, inciting a chuckle from Fayina.

Before heading west to the front, they would travel southeast for training at Engels. Over the eight day train ride, they would meet their fellow recruits and hear their stories, and attempt to make their uniforms fit. Working as a seamstress, Lilia's mother had taught her to cut and sew on the family's sewing machine. She drew new patterns on the pieces of her uniform, knowing well how to cut and sew them back together. The steam train chugged away toward Engels as the girls chatted, in excitement, and nervousness of what lay ahead.

Across from Lilia, sat Katya Budanova, tall and lean, with dark hair. She was older than the others, and serious. After Katya's father had died, she was sent to Moscow to join her sister. She had found work in an aircraft factory, and flown in air parades over Moscow. Two months prior, Katya's sister had returned to Smolensk to visit their mother when the air raids had started. They were awakened just before dawn to the terrifying scream of a Ju-87 dive-bomber, known as the Stuka, followed by an explosion nearby. Katya's mother and sister scrambled to gather what belongings they could to head for the safety of the east. The Luftwaffe would drop just enough bombs to cause the mass evacuation of entire villages, a tactic that created their real target, main roads swollen with refugees.

Katya's sister and mother had made it out of their village, onto a main road toward Moscow. They soon found themselves caught in a slow-moving mass of trucks, donkey carts, and refugees on foot. They again heard the rumble of airplane engines overhead. Then came the screech of a dozen Stukas. Bombs landed in the midst of refugees, a blistering chaos of mass death. Katya's sister had run to the side of the road and jumped into a ditch moments before a Heinkel ground attack plane passed, strafing the road. She watched helpless as bullets ripped through her mother, the plane roaring overhead. She climbed out of the ditch to reach her mother lying dead, along with hundreds of others. In an instant another plane appeared, firing its guns, leaving Katya's sister dead next to her mother. The road was reduced to a smoking tangle of carnage and blood. A neighbor from her village had witnessed the attack and managed to survive. After completing the long walk to Moscow, he found Katya and relayed the terrible news. A powerful motivation now burned inside of her, revenge. Learning of the female regiments, Katya was eager to join. Lilia watched Katya curiously as she struggled with the needle and thread, and pulling too hard on a stitch, it broke.

"Do you need some help?" Lilia offered, quietly, sensing the rage inside of her.

Katya looked up to see Lilia's face. "I'm good with an airplane. Not so good with a needle and thread," she said, looking over Lilia's uniform. "Looks like you know what you're doing there."

"My mother is a seamstress," Lilia replied. "It's an unfair advantage."

"Then, yes. I suppose I could use some help," Katya conceded.

The steam train rumbled on through the night to Engels. As Lilia showed Katya how to properly fit her uniform and finish off the stitches, Katya told her of the fate of her mother and sister, and of her burning desire to wipe the fascist invaders from the country, a sentiment shared by all. Lilia tried to sleep when the sewing was done, but her thoughts kept her awake. How could the whole world have changed so much, and so quickly? Her country was fighting for its own survival and she would soon be in the middle of it all.

While the train slowly made its way to Engels, idle countryside passed outside the train cars. Four days into the journey, the train stopped on the tracks, waiting for an interchange. Another train heading in the opposite direction moved slowly past. It was filled with young men in uniform heading for the front. Katya and the others rushed to the window to call out to them.

"Death to the fascists!" Katya shouted. "Save our Motherland, boys!"

They looked out, smiling and shouting at the sudden sight of women in uniform, a brief exchange in the seconds while the cars passed. In a moment their train began to move again and the moment was gone. The soldiers on the passing train were being delivered directly to the front line.

On the first day at the training facility in Engels, the female recruits were ushered into a barber station. Tears were shed as their long hair dropped to the floor one by one until it was Lilia's turn.

"No," Lilia said calmly. "You needn't bother, my hair is already at the right length for my look." Lilia had carefully styled her hair like the famous actress Valentina Serova had styled it in her most recent film, and was often complimented and told they looked alike. Yet the Secretary of the Party Organization to the Regiment, Klavdiya Terekhova, had been given her instructions to carry out. She returned to Marina Raskova, telling her that the hair of every recruit had been cut short but Lilia.

"Then you haven't carried out my order!" Raskova barked at her. Raskova knew that her first task in transforming the girls into soldiers was to get them to look like soldiers, stripped of civilian attitudes. Klavdiya returned to Lilia in tears.

"Please, Lilia. You must." Amidst the stares of other recruits, Lilia finally agreed.

With her hair cut short, Lilia looked even more demure. She was shorter than all the others but one.

"It will grow back," a voice behind her spoke. Lilia turned to see Antonina Lebedeva. With their short, sandy blonde hair, both of them little more than five feet tall, they could have been twins.

"I know," Lilia said, studying Antonina.

"Antonina." She offered.

"Lilia," she replied.

Like Katya, Antonina had also lost her family at the front. She had been enrolled in the aviation institute in Moscow when the war started. Her family and everyone she had known from childhood were gone. She had been amongst the first to write letters asking to join the army as a pilot. Eventually, her letters found their way to Marina Raskova. She was among the first to sign up, qualifying for fighters with an impressive number of hours in the air. Lilia studied Antonina, learning bits of her story, and the fate of her family. Yet Lilia wondered to herself if Antonina was somehow too gentle of a soul to be a true killer at the front. Then it occurred to Lilia that she might give others the same impression. What else was Antonina to do, but to use her precious skill to fight for the motherland with her comrades, to fight for what was left?

A week into training, the female recruits were issued winter uniforms, overcoats and fur lined boots, and again they were all too big, as they had been intended for men. When they lined up before Marina Raskova the following afternoon for inspection, an Aide de Camp moved down the line looking over the recruits, all standing rigidly at attention. He stopped before a recruit.

"Your trousers are to be tucked into your boots, not left sagging over the top." The Aide de Camp barked.

"Yes, comrade Captain," she quickly replied.

He continued on, stopping squarely in front of Lilia, a stern expression growing across his face. As the other recruits stood in line, their uniforms too big for them, their feet in oversized boots, Lilia stood with a fitting uniform that showed off her figure, and around her collar was white fur, taken from the inside of her boots.

"What is the meaning of this?" he said sternly. "Litvyak, why are you the only one here with a fur collar?" He continued.

"Doesn't it improve the look?" Lilia replied.

"The purpose of a uniform is to be just that, uniform!" He said angrily.

Marina Raskova stepped forward.

"Litvyak, you will spend the night under arrest, returning your uniform to its proper condition," Raskova stated firmly. "Take her away."

Fayina Pleshivtseva stood in line with the others, watching as Lilia was taken to a jail cell for the night. '*What is this ridiculous girl thinking?*' Fayina thought to herself. Didn't she realize what was ahead? How could she be worried about fashion when there was a war to be fought? But Lilia had caught her attention. In the weeks that followed, Fayina would watch as Lilia made her flights over the airfield, and witness her skills in the air. She couldn't yet know how much her and Lilia's lives would intertwine.

Chapter 3

Stanislav Zuchenko shivered in his bed. The nightmares had returned. His mind was overwhelmed with snarling wolves, running in a pack through a forest blanketed in snow, accompanied by the feeling of absolute fear. He woke suddenly, looking around at the safety of his Moscow apartment and the steel grey sky that hung over the city outside. Each day began the same for him, not recollecting what had stirred him awake, yet drenched in the feeling that he had just escaped a terrible end. It was January of 1942. On that particular morning he sat up and opened a small cabinet next to his bed, and took out a small medical kit with a syringe and an ampule of morphine. He tied a strip of cloth over his arm, just above the elbow, to fatten the veins. A quick plunge of the needle, and the opiate calm washed over him, settling his mind and dispatching the anxiety of his nightmare. He washed and dressed himself, putting on the freshly pressed and starched uniform befitting his rank of Colonel in the NKVD. He buttoned his cuffs and straightened his jacket, smoothing every wrinkle. He understood the importance of looking every bit the part he was to play in Soviet society. He put on the blue cap, looking himself over in the mirror, setting it perfectly straight on his head.

In the years before the October revolution, Stanislav Zuchenko had been seduced by the ideas that would give it strength. Though the revolution itself was messy, he clung to the idea of what was possible on the other side. The Tsars and their five children had all been executed, the past order destroyed so that the future could be born. It was his fervent belief that the momentum of history could be outpaced. The future must be better than the past, and so would being part of a collective, compared to the hard life he had known as a child. In the new society, every person would think for the good of society itself, and what followed would be a new age that was greater than the sum of its parts. When true communism was finally achieved, there would exist a state of pure egalitarian brotherhood. Everyone would be given a new heart, and achieve a new state of enlightenment. The very nature of man would evolve into a new type of person, unburdened by the old ways of thinking. The New Soviet Man and the New Soviet Woman would emerge to build a society of perpetual progress.

With his belief in the doctrines of collectivism, and his contributions to the revolution, Stanislav Zuchenko had risen through the ranks of the Communist Party, and the NKVD. He had managed to keep his position even while several heads of the NKVD and colleagues around him had played out their roles, only to be replaced and frog-marched into the basement of the Lubyanka Prison and executed themselves. Two decades after the Revolution, the Secretary General of the Communist

Party, Joseph Stalin, had built around himself a cult of personality so complete it was hard to imagine a time when anyone could have looked up to the Tsars. He had gathered a collective of authors and artists to gain complete control over any published work, and personally signed off on any film script. No film could be shown without first gaining the clearance of the Kremlin. Vladimir Lenin and Leon Trotsky were both edited out of a film about the October Revolution by Sergei Eisenstein. History was rewritten to show that it was Stalin alone who had led the revolution. To be certain it would not haunt him, an assassin was dispatched to find Trotsky in Mexico and have his death delivered by an ice axe to the skull. The NKVD had become Stalin's most important tool in keeping an iron grip on power and continually building his image in the minds of the Soviet people.

By the winter of 1942, the German Army would come to within 20 kilometers of Moscow. The exceptionally cold winter froze their gasoline, stopping tanks and trucks, bringing the offensive to a standstill. If the tide of the war was to change, there was no time to spare. Stanislav Zuchenko knew it would take more than the sheer number of troops sent to the front, it would take complete and total belief in the Soviet system, the Communist Party, and in Stalin himself as savior of the Motherland.

As Colonel Zuchenko entered the door to his office, he was quickly followed by his Adjunct, Grigor, who carried a sealed letter. He offered the letter urgently.

"A communiqué from the Secretary General, comrade," said Grigor as he handed over the letter then took a step back to wait as it was opened and read. Stanislav took a seat at his desk to examine the letter more closely. At the bottom was the signature of Secretary General Stalin himself. He was to be given the task of personally overseeing news of the newly formed female air regiments. They would get their chance to fight at the front alongside the men, but Stanislav knew immediately that their real value to the war effort was far greater than any achievement in battle. They would serve as inspiration to the soldiers fighting on the ground, and to the workers in munitions factories behind them.

Stanislav turned to Grigor. "Ready the car," he said. "We are going to Engels to visit the women's air regiments."

At the training camp in Engels, Lilia found herself in the cockpit of a Yakovlev series-1 fighter plane. It was an awesome machine compared with the slow-moving biplanes she had learned to fly at the air club. It was a sleek, fast airplane, capable of almost 500 kilometers per hour that could climb to over 10,000 meters. Built on a steel and wood airframe, machine guns were built into the wings, and a 20mm cannon fired high explosive ammunition from the nose of the airplane, mounted between the cylinder banks of the massive twelve cylinder engine that turned out over 1,100 horsepower. Lilia would test the limits of the new airplane as she had the biplanes at the air club, and the Yak-1 would respond with incredible power and speed. Blocks of wood had to be fixed to the pedals so Lilia could reach them. Lilia and the other female pilots practiced mock dogfights. They would meet in mid-air and attempt to outmaneuver each other to gain the advantage. In the years before the war, Lilia had developed a reputation at the air club as a daredevil pilot, always pushing herself and the biplanes to the limit. In the Yak-1, she would employ all of her skills, impressing Commander Raskova in the process. She had also learned to fire the guns with a button on the control stick, with target practice on a dummy plane towed by a cable behind a PO-2 biplane. The skill she had to master was to hit a moving target from a moving platform, matching the speed and direction of the bullets with the speed and direction of the target.

When Colonel Zuchenko arrived at Engels, Lilia was in the air in her Yak-1 in a mock dogfight. He heard the roar of the powerful Yak-1 engines above as he stepped out of the black sedan. The camp was abuzz with activities, airplanes in mock dogfights above the base, while future ground crew learned how to properly pack parachutes and re-arm and refuel the planes. An Aide de Camp of the base looked at Colonel Zuchenko's uniform and offered a salute, then led him to Major Raskova. Engines buzzing in the sky above, Zuchenko stood next to Marina Raskova, watching carefully as Lilia flipped the fighter plane into a tight turn, followed by a snap roll, putting her directly behind her opponent.

"Who is flying up there?" he asked Major Raskova.

"Nechayeva and Litvyak," she replied.

"And which is the one giving chase?" he pressed.

"Litvyak," Raskova replied.

"She seems quite skilled."

Raskova nodded with a smile, knowing the Colonel was witnessing one of her best pilots in action. Zuchenko took a small notebook and pencil from his coat pocket and entered a single word note, '*Litvyak.*' He continued to stare into the sky, impressed, and even inspired. Was he bearing witness to the promised future, the New Soviet Woman?

The following day, the one thousand female recruits gathered inside a hangar at the Engels training camp, lined up in perfect rows for their graduation ceremony. Their uniforms now fit, and their hair had grown back. While Lilia had spent most of the past six months at Engels learning to dogfight in the Yak-1, Fayina had been in a classroom and workshops, learning the specifics of the Yak-1's engine and various systems, and how to fix them, as it would be her responsibility at the front to keep an airplane ready for flight. Marina Raskova stood before a podium, an enormous portrait of Joseph Stalin hung behind her from floor to ceiling. Colonel Zuchenko stood by the hangar door smoking a cigarette as she read off the names of pilots, giving official assignments to each of three regiments. The 586th was the designation for the fighter regiment. The pilots of the 587th would fly in bombers by day. The 588th night bombers would fly PO-2 biplanes by night, dropping bombs on German airfields causing destruction and giving their pilots sleepless nights. At the front they would earn the name Nachthexen, German for Night Witches.

"The following pilots have qualified and will be assigned to the fighter regiment designated five eighty-sixth I.A.P.," said Raskova proudly, and then spoke the names. "...Polyantseva... Budanova..."

Katya was unable to contain her smile, knowing she would get the chance to avenge her family.

"...Khomyakova... Belayeva... Kuznetsova... Prokorova... Glukovtseva... Lebedeva... Litvyak... Nechayeva..." Raskova continued, as a wide smile crossed Lilia's face.

When all the names had been read, all the recruits gave a loud cheer. They milled in the hangar, congratulating their comrades. Katya embraced Lilia.

"We made it!" Katya said, and then let go her embrace. "I'll see you at the celebration. I've got to congratulate some of the others."

As Katya stepped away, Fayina approached Lilia. "I've been given my assignment, Lilia," she said, "I'm to be your mechanic," then stood at attention to salute, "Mechanic Pleshivtseva, reporting for duty."

Lilia smiled and embraced Fayina. At that moment Lilia caught sight of Colonel Zuchenko, watching her from the corner of the hangar. For half a second their eyes met. The sight of his uniform gave her a chill. Lilia kept the smile on her face and quickly looked away.

"Off to the front we go," Lilia said, then turned her eyes again to see that Colonel Zuchenko was gone. A crushed cigarette butt smoldered on the floor where he had stood.

The next morning Lilia, Katya, and the other pilots of the 586th were moved to their new assignment at Saratov, across the Volga River from Engels. Their primary mission would be the protection of fixed targets, in particular the Yakovlev aircraft factory, a potential target well away from the front. As they settled into the barracks and the daily routine of patrol flights over Saratov, they grew restless.

It was the summer of 1942. Lilia sat in the cockpit of her Yak-1 fighter plane, camouflage green, numbered in white 23, at the end of the runway. Katya sat in the cockpit of her own Yak-1, numbered 44 in yellow, parked next to Lilia, both awaiting orders. They had been stationed in Saratov for over a month, far away from the front. Lilia took a pencil and paper from the pocket of her flight suit and wrote a letter to her mother:

> "Dearest Mamushka, I am on scramble alert today and have spent most of the day in my aircraft, not having flown a single mission. During these hard times, we are leading a life of leisure; meanwhile, our tired out male regiments could use such a rest. Virtually no one amongst us wants to live in wartime as peacefully as we do now. All of us are thirsting for battle, especially me..."

Lilia wrote amidst the sounds of birds and insects, and peaceful countryside.

At night the women of the 586th would retire to the barracks, where amidst the rows of bunks, they would sing, gossip, and tell stories.

Katya sat in her bunk, reading to Lilia an account of an air battle over the front.

"Another cannon shot from Captain Solomatin destroyed the last Messerschmitt. With only seven of their own planes, they defended against twenty-five enemy fighters without losing a single plane, for the enemy's loss of twelve." Katya looked up to Lilia, marveling at the story. "Twenty-five against seven."

"Command would rather send seven against twenty-five than let us near the front," Lilia replied.

"We'll get our chance to fight," uttered a voice confidently. Lilia and Katya turned to see that it was Antonina Lebedeva, followed by Fayina. Antonina twirled before them, wearing a brassiere with a distinctive red stripe across one side. "What do you think?" she asked. "Fayina made it out of parachute silk. I think it will hold up in flight."

"Why are you making brassieres for Antonina?" Lilia said. "You're supposed to be my mechanic."

"Because she asked," Fayina replied. "I can make one for you too."

Since their arrival three months prior, the 586th passed the summer of 1942 in relative calm at Saratov. Further down the Volga, in mid-July, the battle for Stalingrad had begun.

Back in his office at NKVD headquarters in Moscow, Stanislav Zuchenko followed daily reports of the battles at the front line, which now stretched some 2,800 kilometers. His Adjunct, Grigor, had delivered the reports early that day, and stood in Zuchenko's office awaiting further instructions. The Colonel looked through the reports and the news they conveyed. The assault on Stalingrad was underway. A force of more than 400,000 German troops had advanced on the city with 300 tanks and 2,000 guns and mortars, against the out-numbered Red Army. He sat back in his chair contemplating the news.

"What's next?" asked Grigor.

"We are losing twenty thousand men every day at the front," Zuchenko said grimly. "What do men have to push them forward in the face of certain death?" he contemplated aloud. "William Shakespeare wrote that 'All the world is a stage, and we are merely its players.' We are on the world's stage now, Grigor, and everyone is watching to see the fate of the world decided in this fight for Stalingrad. We must give the people courage, so that our soldiers fight on, and our nation survive." he continued.

"A visit to the 586th at Saratov. That is what is next."

Stanislav Zuchenko had learned his craft under the old Bolsheviks in the Department of Agitation and Propaganda. He had learned to be effective in writing speeches, printing fly-ers, and most importantly-crafting the stories and phrases that would stir people to action. To make the most of his position and resources, he would need stories of his female pilots in combat. He believed they could be his greatest tool of all to win the hearts of the Russian people, and to urge the soldiers on to fight.

It was late August of 1942. Fayina had gotten hold of a set of paints and brushes. She stood on a step stool painting an insignia on the side of Lilia's airplane. It was the sketch of a white flower, a lily.

"What do you think?" Fayina said, as she stepped down and looked over her work.

Lilia looked it over and a grin came across her face. "Perfect."

The paint was still wet on Lilia's insignia when Colonel Zuchenko arrived at the airfield. On the long drive to Saratov he flipped through his notebook, finding on a page the name he had written three months prior, 'Litvyak.' After finding Lilia's aircraft, he stood a moment to stare at the lily on its side, the paint still drying. Lilia walked around the tail of her airplane to find Zuchenko staring at it. She stopped quickly, recognizing his uniform. As he turned to notice her, she quickly saluted.

"Sergeant Litvyak, I presume?"

"Yes, Comrade Colonel." she replied.

He looked her over curiously. It was the first time they had spoken. If Stanislav Zuchenko had known the details of Vladimir Litvyak's arrest, he would have had to carry out Stalin's executive order 'No 1926SS on *Family Members of Traitors of the Motherland*' signed only two months earlier, and had Lilia sent immediately to a labor camp. But the sheer volume of paperwork from the later days of the Purge had overwhelmed the paperwork from its early days. Vladimir Litvyak's case file, the details of his arrest, trial and execution, and his designation as an 'Enemy of the People' had been buried in the archive under nearly a million other case files. The name Litvyak was otherwise unknown to him.

"It's a pleasure to meet you," he said. "I am Colonel Stanislav Zuchenko. I've heard a lot about your flying." He returned his attention to the flower painted on the side of her plane with a grin. "Very interesting. It's a lily isn't it, for your name? Was this your idea?"

"Yes, Comrade Colonel."

"What shall our enemy think when they see it?" he continued.

"I doubt we'll see much of the enemy this far from the front," Lilia replied.

"You would prefer to be closer? To get into the fight?" Zuchenko asked calmly.

"Yes, Comrade Colonel," she answered.

"More fascists to shoot at, I suppose. It's a nasty business at the front, seeing the enemy nearly every day, to see your comrades killed or injured, or even be killed yourself. Is that really what you want?" he asked.

"I joined to fight, Comrade Colonel." Lilia replied.

"A girl who paints flowers on her plane that can shoot down the fascists as well as the men," he said, contemplating it. He took another look at the insignia of the white lily before replying, "I'll see what arrangements can be made."

Stanislav Zuchenko nodded, turned, and walked away. The deal was struck.

Chapter 4

On the 10th of September, 1942, three days after Colonel Zuchenko's visit to the 586th, Lilia Litvyak, Katya Budanova, Raisa Belayeva, and Mariya Kuznetsova were called forward during the morning meeting and given new orders. They were to be reassigned to the 437th flying regiment, an all male unit currently operating over Stalingrad. The four women gathered together and stepped aside, no longer pilots of the 586th. They said goodbye to their fellow pilots with a mix of anxious energy and excitement, knowing what it meant. They would get their chance to face the enemy over the front.

Lilia, Katya, Raisa, and Mariya laid a map on the tail wing of Katya's Yak-1 fighter plane, plotting their route to the new airbase. They would fly in a formation of four, following the Volga River 320 kilometers south to Stalingrad, then find the airbase east of the city. Ground support crews would arrive later by truck. They folded up the map, climbed into their airplanes, and readied for take off. Word had travelled quickly through the base that the four pilots were being sent to the front. The other pilots, mechanics, and ground crew all stopped for a moment to watch the four Yak-1s paused at the end of the runway, waving as they took to the sky, on their way to Stalingrad. Fayina worked busily loading tools and equipment onto a truck, preparing to follow.

The four Yaks held formation over the Volga, matching airspeed, with Raisa in the lead. In just under an hour, the city of Stalingrad came into view. Their first sight was a massive column of black smoke rising into the sky from the still burning oil depot. As they got closer, the sight of Stalingrad grew more nightmarish. Just two and a half weeks of fighting had devastated the city. Most of the buildings were bombed in half, or completely to rubble. Boats filled with Russian soldiers made the dangerous crossing of the Volga under artillery fire. The average life expectancy of a Russian soldier on the ground was less than a day. Lilia and Katya both stared at the city in awe as they flew closer to the destruction. Before the Yaks reached the city, Raisa waggled her wings, and turned the formation east to find their new airbase. She navigated the route, noting landmarks to guide them to the airfield. At mid-morning the four Yaks landed at the 437th and taxied to the side of the runway.

Lilia pulled back her canopy and stepped down onto the wing. Looking around, the base was frantic with activity. A male pilot, looking exhausted, ran past her to climb into his plane, he stared curiously at her without time to talk. As he strapped himself in and started the plane, he caught for just a moment the image of the white lily painted on the fuselage Lilia's airplane. He stared for a moment, while the ground crew turned his plane around by the tail section putting it out of view. The propeller sped up as he taxied to the end of the runway and just as quickly took off, returning to the fight.

"Excuse me," Lilia called out to an armorer rushing past her with a cart of ammunition. He looked at her quizzically as he kept moving. It seemed that for everyone at the base, every second counted, and not one could be wasted.

Lilia looked to her side to see Katya, Raisa and Mariya standing next to her watching the rush of pilots, armorers and ground crews. Pilots ran to strap themselves into returning planes, yelling to the ground crews to get them in the air.

"They don't seem to notice us," Lilia said.

"They're in the fight, Lilia," said Katya, aloud. "Everyone here is in the fight."

Katya stepped forward and yelled to an older male mechanic. "Hey, you," she said, demanding his full attention. "Where can we find the commanding officer of this base?"

He stopped, awed at the sight of four female pilots in uniforms, then raised an arm and pointed to the command bunker.

Lilia and the others walked down the steps into the darkness of the bunker, lit by lanterns hanging on posts. Noises of the airfield, airplane engines and the rumbling of bombs in the distance were silenced, replaced by frantic voices as the officers assessed the dire situation. Half of their planes had already been lost defending the city. As Lilia, Katya, Raisa, and Mariya approached, a beleaguered Colonel looked up from his desk.

"Reporting for duty," Katya said. "We've come to join the fight."

He sat back astonished, looking them over. "It's come to this already?" he said to no one in particular, unenthusiastic at the prospect of putting women into frontline combat. "You are the pilots from the 586th?" he continued.

"Yes, sir," Lilia replied.

"Inform me when your ground crew arrives. That is all for now," said the Colonel. "Show them to their quarters." He waived to an aide.

For the next two days, they would wait on the sidelines of the bloodiest battle in human history. The male pilots would huddle to eat a meal after dark, exhausted by a full day of fighting, faces covered in oil and dirt. They talked of aerial maneuvers used successfully in combat. On their second day at the base, Lilia and Katya witnessed a pilot return with barely enough energy to land the plane, and just enough to pull himself from the cockpit, climb down from the wing before falling to his knees next to the plane, and finally lying down flat on the runway altogether. A ground crewman and a fellow pilot picked him up by the shoulders and carried him to a cot to recover.

"Come on, Ivan. You did well," the other pilot said as he dragged him away. Though the pilot had returned his aircraft to the base unharmed, it was well understood the physical strain of a sustained dogfight. The mental focus and surging adrenaline in a fight for one's life could push the human body to its absolute limit.

For his victory the ground crew had painted a small red star on the side of his plane. It was a sliver of hope amidst otherwise grim news, when losses had far outnumbered victories day after day. By evening the pilot had recovered enough strength to recount the days' events. The other pilots fell silent over their meals that evening as he described the battle in detail. Lilia and Katya sat quietly, listening to the account. He had been caught in a fight with two Messerschmitt bf 109s just outside the city. It had taken every bit of strength and focus to avoid the gunfire of the two enemy fighters and escape with his life. The three planes had been locked in an ever-tightening turn, all the while losing altitude. To break out of the carousel would mean certain death. His only chance was to hold the turn and hope to outlast his opponents in the deadly game of aerial chess. Looking above his canopy he had seen the faces of his two opponents and described them. The pilot in the lead was older, more experienced and methodical. The other was younger and less steady, offering him a lucky break when he almost collided with the lead fighter in his eagerness to put the guns on him. The enemy pilot had pulled away quickly to avoid the collision, briefly exposing himself. Ivan fired a machine gun burst that shredded his left wing. The enemy fighter fell sideways and crashed in flames. With one opponent left, he held the lighter Yak-1 in a tighter turn, clipping a few rounds into the tail section of the remaining Messerschmitt. Assessing his losing situation, the older pilot pulled a surprise diving split-S and broke out of the fight, escaping to the west.

The other pilots sat in rapt attention as Ivan finished his tale. He recalled the look he had seen on the downed pilots face, gnashing his teeth in anticipation of taking his life. Although the young pilot had beaten his opponents, he took no joy in the victory. He had finally seen the face of the enemy, and it was the face of hatred.

"It will never be enough for these men to simply defeat us," he said with profound sadness. "They would destroy us all to the very last woman and child. Why?" He wondered aloud.

Another pilot broke the silence. "You beat them, Ivan. Outnumbered and you beat them," he said, putting a hand on the younger man's shoulder. "We'll keep beating them until this war is won."

Vodka was poured into glasses and passed around the room. The older pilot handed a glass to Ivan, urging him to take it, then raised his glass. "To your victory against the fascists."

All together, the other pilots raised their glasses and cheered. "Urrahh!" then drank.

Katya held up her glass and followed suit. "Urrahh!"

On the morning of September 13, 1942, Raisa announced to the regiment Colonel that the four women's Yak fighters were ready for combat. They stood before him awaiting orders.

"You're on standby," the Colonel replied.

The battle for Stalingrad had raged for three weeks, in close combat fighting on the ground, with house-to-house battles and massive civilian casualties. For a soldier on the ground, the sound of battle was terrifying by itself. There was the constant popping of machine gun fire, the roar of the Stukas, and the concussion of bombshells exploding nearby. Above the city, was heard the shrieking of airplane engines and the gunfire of daily air battles, and all around the cries in agony of the wounded and dying.

Lilia sat in her cockpit in anticipation of what was to come. With every second that passed, she steeled her nerves, fully alert, keeping calm in anticipation. Every thought must be focused, every action deliberate. She could be face to face with the enemy in a matter of minutes. She had reached the battlefront and now everything was on the line, her family name as well as her life.

"Be strong Lilia," she told herself. "You can outfly them all."

Moments later a call came across the radio. The radio operator quickly ran over to relay the message.

"Bombers spotted inbound, one hundred Kilometers northwest of the city! Altitude five thousand meters."

Two flares shot up over the end of the runway. Lilia, Katya, Raisa, and Mariya quickly started their engines, their propellers spinning into a blur. The four Yaks taxied down the runway, picking up speed. The nose of Raisa's Yak, in the lead, dipped and the wheels lifted off the runway, followed by

Mariya, Katya, and Lilia. Climbing into the sky, they moved into formation, gaining altitude. Raisa lead the formation higher to meet the bombers from above as a tactical advantage, pushing the Yaks to their maximum ceiling. Raisa waggled her wings, then put on her oxygen mask, motioning the other pilots to do the same.

The four Yak fighters crossed over the north end of Stalingrad, past the massive column of black smoke, still gaining altitude. They climbed through a light cloud layer, gaining full view of the horizon. Lilia was the first to spot the formation of bombers in the distance. She waggled her wings to get the others attention, then pointed low and to the right. A formation of eight bombers making a run toward Stalingrad. Raisa adjusted course and the others followed to intercept the enemy planes. Dark specks on the horizon were fast approaching with a combined speed of close to 1,000 kilometers per hour.

Lilia unlocked her gun trigger and put a finger on it to reacquaint herself with the mechanism, switching between the 20mm cannon that fired through the nose cone of the fighter and the machine guns mounted in the wings. The gap was closing in a matter of heartbeats. Raisa made the first break in a sharp turn to dive toward the lead bomber. She opened a machine gun blast, raking bullets across the wing as she dove through the formation behind the leader. Lilia followed, pushing the stick forward, putting her fighter into a steep dive toward the point of intercept ahead of the bomber. Calculating the precise point where her bullets could meet the bombers right engine, closing in and gaining speed, flashes of gunfire erupted from the upper turret of the JU-88, streaking bullets past her canopy. Lilia switched to the 20mm cannon and pulled the trigger three times. Her third shot set the bomber's right engine on fire as she dove through the formation. Black smoke and flames streaked into the sky from the crippled bomber. An explosion split its wing, causing it to drop sideways out of the formation. Lilia spotted Raisa below the formation making a tight turn in the nimble Yak-1 to make another pass at the slower Junckers 88s. The other bombers began to scatter, dropping their bombs to lose weight and make a faster getaway. Lilia lost track of Katya and Mariya making their own passes on the scattering pack.

Raisa climbed in a tight turn, firing machine guns, raking the fuselage of a quickly passing bomber. After passing the bomber, gunfire streaked across Raisa's right wing. Two Messerschmitt bf109 fighter planes flying high cover attacked, turning onto Raisa's tail. The chaos of the battle had turned in an instant, and suddenly they were up against German fighters that were near their equal in speed and maneuverability. The dogfight had begun. Raisa realized her situation and turned hard left. The Messerschmitt overshot her position, then turned hard to chase.

Lilia spotted Raisa in danger with two Messerschmitt on her tail and kicked the pedals in a fast turn and dive behind them. She fired a machine gun burst, punching holes in the wing of the Messerschmitt in the rear. The pilot broke hard right and out of the fight while the lead Messerschmitt kept on Raisa's tail trying to get a shot. Lilia fired another machine gun burst at the remaining Messerschmitt, glancing bullets off the fuselage, getting the pilots full attention. He broke hard in an attempt to get around on Lilia.

Raisa turned hard, trying to put herself behind the Messerschmitt that was chasing her. She pressed her gun button but nothing came out. In her eager passes on the bombers she had used all of her ammunition. Now out of ammunition and of no use, Raisa put her fighter in a dive and pushed full throttle back toward base.

Lilia was alone in the sky, locked in battle with a determined German pilot of considerable skill, and an aircraft equal to her own. Lilia pulled her fighter plane into a tight turn, matching speed and engaging in the deadly fight. As she did so, she spotted the markings on the enemy pilot's tail and fuselage denoting his many previous kills. He was an ace from the famous Richtofen Fighter Group, which carried the legacy of Manfred Von Richtofen who had become known as the Red Baron. In his signature bright red tri-plane, he was considered the deadliest pilot of the First World War. Lilia knew that a single wrong move could cost her life.

The German pilot put his aircraft into a series of skids and rolls attempting to put himself on Lilia's tail. She countered with her own maneuvers, adjusting the throttle, and kicking the airplane into rolls and skids. The two fighter planes grappled in a fast, rolling duel, moving in opposing corkscrews, each pilot pushing their plane to its limit. Speed, maneuverability, and skill would determine the difference between life and death.

The German pilot made a surprise move with a fast pitch back and roll, expecting to catch his unknown rival by surprise and put himself on Lilia's tail position. She quickly countered, breaking hard right, catching the German ace at the bottom of his maneuver, right behind his tail and pulled the trigger, letting out a rattle of gunfire into his wings and tail section.

The German Pilot tried to break out of his position to find that his aircraft had lost the function of its tail wings, the controls barely responding. Lilia held her position. As she readied to fire another burst of gunfire, she saw the tattered fighter plane's canopy open. The German pilot unbuckled his harness and pulled the stick hard over left, flipping the Messerschmitt upside down. The pilot dropped into the sky, his crippled fighter plane heading toward the ground with a trail of white smoke.

Lilia circled around to see a bloom of white parachute silk open in the sky below. A rush of exhilaration came over her. She had won the fight, and proved herself in the skies over Stalingrad. Somewhere inside the adrenaline, she felt a tinge of sadness. She had downed the bomber and scattered the formation, and beaten one of the Luftwaffe's best fighter pilots, yet there was a realization. How had the world come to this? They were pilots too, even if they were the enemy. At that moment Lilia could have circled around and shot her rival helpless in his parachute, and in so doing break an unwritten code of honor. She pulled the stick gently and turned her fighter plane back to base.

Raisa met Lilia as she stepped down from the wing of her aircraft, berating herself that in her overzealousness in the bomber attacks she had used up all of her ammunition. Katya and Mariya had also returned to the base and waited anxiously for Lilia to compare the details of their encounter.

Lilia touched down and was then debriefed by the airbase's commanding officer who wrote up the details of the air battle and entered it into the official record. Fayina took out a set of paints and a brush, and next to the lily painted on the fuselage, she stenciled on two small red stars, one for each victory. After more than a year in the single-minded anticipation of what it would be like to face the enemy in the sky, she had finally passed the veil of the great unknown.

That evening, pilots of the regiment had gathered in the command bunker and talked of the day's events when a vehicle pulled to a stop outside the bunker. The airbase commander heard a commotion and stepped outside to find two Russian soldiers holding a German pilot in uniform at gunpoint, and motioned for him to step down.

"And what is this?" said the airbase commander.

"We picked him up north of Stalingrad. He bailed out of a Messerschmitt one-o-nine," replied a soldier. "Your unit had the only record of a downed Messer in the area today."

"Bring him in," replied the commander.

The German pilot was slightly older than the other pilots in the room. His expression was stoic, realizing the danger he was in and that mercy was unlikely. He straightened his uniform, attempting to maintain some of his pride.

The commander set out a chair and instructed the German pilot to sit. He then turned to his aide, "Go and get Staff Sergeant Litvyak."

The German pilot sat nervously as his Russian counterparts looked him over, studying the iron cross and oak leaves medals around his neck and his neatly pressed uniform. They all understood they were not in the presence of an ordinary pilot, but an ace.

The airbase commander calmly told his aide, "Ask him if he would like to meet the pilot who shot him down," who then turned and asked the question in German.

The German ace sat back hesitantly, then nodded and replied in German.

The commander's aide translated, "He says he would very much like to meet the pilot. He must surely be one of our best." The pilots smiled, containing themselves.

Moments later, Lilia entered the bunker. She looked over the German pilot. Not knowing what to make of the scene, she turned to the airbase commander.

"You called for me, Commander?"

"Yes, it's about the Messer you shot down today," he said, then pointed to the German sitting in a chair in the middle of the room. "This is the pilot."

Lilia paused, looking him over, now face to face. The German pilot stared back at Lilia and the other pilots in the room, then shrugged.

The Commander's Aide explained in German, "Sie ist der Pilot."

The German pilot scowled at the small blonde girl before him, only five feet tall, with blue-grey eyes, then exclaimed loudly "Das ist unmöglich!" 'It's impossible!' He said, offended to be made the butt of a Russian joke.

"What did he say?" Lilia asked the Commander's Aide.

"He doesn't believe you are the pilot that shot him down," he replied, reluctantly.

The statement aroused in her a moment of contempt. She stared at the German pilot and then stepped back. She held up her hands and began to describe the details of their encounter. She became more animated with every move, describing their battle in detail. She rolled her right hand palm over then formed it into a gun, aiming it at her left hand to describe his ultimate mistake. "And then, I shot you out of the sky," she finished.

The rival pilot's expression changed. Only the pilot who had beaten him could have known the exact details of their duel. He hung his head, finally conceding, then nodded with respect, "Ja, sie ist der pilot."

The other pilots burst out in raucous cheers in pride for their heroine, Lilia.

Word of the encounter between Lilia and the German Ace was quick to reach Colonel Zuchenko. A young NKVD officer had been present in the bunker amongst the pilots. He had scribbled down the details of the encounter and sent them by messenger to headquarters the next day. Recognizing the opportunity to make the most of her victory, Colonel Zuchenko immediately commissioned an artist to draw a depiction of the scene, and ordered an article written to accompany it. When the drawing was finished, it was of Lilia standing before the older German pilot. The look on his face depicted his previous pride and arrogance being broken, a most feared enemy defeated by a small Russian girl. Colonel Zuchenko smiled, looking over the article and drawing with his Aide looking on.

"This is how we win, Grigor. When the people understand in their hearts what we can accomplish. When we truly ask the most of ourselves..." he said then closed his eyes imagining a grand victory parade with thousands marching proudly under the smiling gaze of Comrade Stalin.

The article and sketch of Lilia's victory and subsequent encounter with the German Ace circulated widely across the front. Colonel Zuchenko considered the real victory to be his own. It was proof the war could be won. Someone who otherwise may have seemed to be one of the weakest and most vulnerable members of Soviet society had risen to defeat one of its fiercest enemies. The article rang out like a clarion call to every soldier at the front and to civilians in the cities, making Lilia something of a living hero. She had come to represent the most precious currency of all to a people fighting for their very survival, hope.

Chapter 5

The day after Lilia's encounter with the German Ace, Katya scored two victories of her own by shooting out the engines of two Junckers-88 bombers outside of Stalingrad. News of her victories had also spread across the front. Both women had earned fame in their first few days of combat. They were both lauded in the press with various articles written and put into circulation across the front and in Moscow.

A week later, the 437th would be re-organized to accommodate aircraft maintenance. While Lilia, Katya, Raisa, and Mariya would keep their Yak-1 fighter planes, the rest of the squadron were to begin flying the Lavochkin-5 that required completely different flight crews to adjust and repair the different avionics and flight systems. It was decided the four women would be transferred to another unit, also flying Yak-1 fighters and operating in the battle for Stalingrad, the elite 9th Guards.

Once again, the women plotted course for a new airbase, climbed into their airplanes and flew off, to be followed by Fayina and other ground crew by truck. Their arrival at the new airbase was vastly different from what they had witnessed at the 437th. The 9th Guards had distinguished themselves in combat, approaching something close to air superiority in their own small corner of the war. After the four women landed and stepped down from their aircraft, they quickly noticed that the ground crews lacked the same frantic hurriedness of the 437th. They worked with focused precision. The pilots of the 9th were among the very best of the Soviet Air Defense, yet they still incurred losses. On the day the four women arrived, they walked across the airfield to witness a group of five pilots just returned from battle. The pilots gathered in a circle near the aircraft lineup a short distance away, with grim expressions on their faces. One pilot pulled out his pistol, raised it in the air, and fired one shot. As the crack of a single pistol shot rang across the airfield, the pilots hung their heads in silence.

"What does it mean?" Lilia asked aloud.

"A pilot has been lost across the line," Katya answered solemnly. "If he survives and is captured he'll be considered a traitor. By Stalin's order, 'there are no prisoners of war, only traitors.' So they are to be forgotten." They had witnessed a funeral in absentia for a fallen comrade.

The pilots then dispersed, ready to receive new orders. Lilia, Katya, Raisa, and Mariya found the command bunker to seek orders of their own. Their arrival at the airbase was seen by the male pilots as a curiosity, and by their commander as a potential distraction. The idea of putting women into combat struck them as abhorrent. The women reported dutifully for three months awaiting front line combat orders that would never be given. Their credentials as pilots with confirmed victories were well known to their fellow male pilots, who treated them respectfully. They were included in nightly discussions of the flight tactics and strategies that would spell the difference between life and death. It was a daily quest at the front line to find every advantage one might have in speed, altitude, or aircraft capability. Yet their assignment to the unit played out as an unspoken conspiracy to keep them away from the most dangerous encounters with the enemy.

Instead of direct engagement with enemy aircraft, they were given missions to escort transport aircraft to frontline positions, with occasional flights of air cover over Stalingrad. They were completing the daily work of combat pilots, even if their assignments were not the most dangerous. After a month of these assignments, and not having fired a single shot, Katya was morose. She wanted nothing less than the whole of her skills turned loose on the enemy daily. As they walked to their bunkers to sleep for the night, she voiced her frustration.

"They treat us like their sisters and daughters, not fellow pilots," said Katya. "We came to fight."

Lilia and the others did not respond, knowing it was true. The pilots of the 9th had grown accustomed to their presence, and with each passing day the idea of their girls being killed or injured in combat grew less palatable. They were a reminder of their wives and daughters at home and everything for which they were fighting. In their minds it was for the men to do the fighting and dying in war.

The four women protested the situation, offering their vodka and chocolate rations to male counterparts for a chance to fly their wing, but found no takers. The impasse was finally broken in early January of 1943 with the arrival of a new fleet of American built Bell P-39 Airacobras, single seat, mid-engine fighter planes built in Buffalo, New York. The airplanes had been built and partially assembled in the New York plant, then taken by rail across Canada and the Alaskan/Canadian Highway. The planes were then shipped across the Bering straight, and further moved by rail across Siberia for final assembly and delivery to the Eastern Front. The male pilots of the 9th Guards were outfitted with the new aircraft while Lilia, Katya, Raisa and Mariya would keep their Soviet built Yak-1 fighters and be transferred yet again. The Soviet pilots of the 9th Guards in their American built fighter planes would go on to become some of the most successful pilots of the war, winning multiple titles of Hero of the Soviet Union. But the four women would not remain with them. Orders came down for Raisa and Mariya to rejoin the female pilots of the 586th, while Lilia and Katya were ordered to another all male regiment, the 296th, also operating outside of Stalingrad.

Once again, Lilia and Katya plotted course for a new airfield. Their fellow pilots offered them fond goodbyes. The women had earned affection and eventually respect from their male counterparts in their time with the 9th Guards, but no new stars on their airplanes. Though the unit had kept their girls from harm out of a sense of chivalry, sidelining experienced and accomplished pilots was a luxury a lesser unit could likely not afford.

Before their departure from the 9th Guards, Lilia and Katya's Yak-1 fighters were outfitted with radios and they had been trained in the use of call signs. Lilia had chosen "Seagull-90", and Katya had chosen "Blackbird-1." They hugged Raisa and Mariya and gave their farewells before watching them take off to return to the 586th, then plotted their own course for the 296th.

With a map spread on the tail wing of her Yak-1, Katya turned to Lilia, wistfully. "You know, we're really a special kind of orphan in this war." Eliciting a chuckle from Lilia.

Further down the Volga river was the airbase of the 296th. Inside its command bunker was Colonel Nikolai Baranov, his face ruddy and weathered beyond his thirty-two years of age. He sat at a desk across from two younger pilots, Aleksei Solomatin, and Alexander "Sasha" Martinov.

"Five pilots, five planes, lost in two weeks," Nikolai Baranov moaned.

"You know what I always say, Kolya. The life of a fighter pilot is like a baby's shirt. It's always too short, and it's soaked in piss." Aleksei responded.

Aleksei had grown cynical since the war had begun. He was one of the few who had survived the initial invasion. His hometown of Kaluga had been occupied by the Germans and had only recently been retaken.

"It gets worse." Nikolai continued, dropping two file folders on the desk, shaking his head. "This is command's idea of replacement pilots," he said, before laying the personnel files for Lilia Litvyak and Katya Budanova on his desk. "Female pilots," Nikolai sighed. "What's next?"

Aleksei picked up a file and opened it. "Lilia..." he said, incredulous.

Sasha picked up the other. "Katya? This must be a joke."

"Shouldn't they be flying transports?" Aleksei asked.

"It's no joke. Their transfer orders are signed by Comrade Stalin himself," said Nikolai.

Colonel Zuchenko had been keeping up to date from afar and had brought the matter to the highest level for approval. Aleksei picked up the transfer order, looking upon the signature curiously. It was indeed the signature of Joseph Stalin. He picked up Lilia's file again.

"She doesn't look like any fighter pilot I've ever seen." said Aleksei. "What are you going to do with them, Kolya?"

"You and Sasha are going to train them." Baranov replied.

"You can't be serious." Aleksei sneered. "We're going to train them and then put them up against the Germans? What chance will they have up there?"

"I am serious. If Stalin says these girls will be flying in my regiment, I'm going to be damn sure they're ready for it." Colonel Baranov's voice boomed across the bunker.

"Aleksei, you'll be flying with Litvyak. Sasha, you'll be flying with Budanova. That is all," he concluded.

Aleksei and Sasha were standing by the row of aircraft, parked on the snow-covered airfield when Lilia and Katya landed at the airbase and taxied their aircraft into the lineup. It was January 8, 1943. Sasha pointed immediately to the lily painted on the side of Lilia's airplane.

"Look at that." Sasha laughed, his breath visible in the cold winter air.

Lilia and Katya quickly climbed down from their cockpits to find Sasha and Aleksei smirking at the painted lily. Sensing she was being mocked, Lilia walked right up to Aleksei.

"Is something funny?" Lilia asked.

"Distract them with the pretty flower, and then move in for the kill. Is that the idea?" Aleksei replied.

Incensed at the remark, Lilia paused, before Katya answered sharply at both of them. "Where can we find the commanding officer of this base?"

Sasha pointed. "In the command bunker. He's right over there. Colonel Nikolai Baranov, a delightful fellow," he told her with a smile.

Lilia gave Aleksei a stern look before she and Katya walked a short distance across the snow to the command bunker. Before Lilia and Katya reached Colonel Baranov's desk, his voice called out from across the bunker.

"Litvyak, Budanova. Come over. Sit down." He said in his deep, imposing voice.

Lilia and Katya calmly sat before him.

"I have your files, and your transfer orders here." Baranov continued. "Saw a bit of action over Stalingrad in September, I see?"

"We each have two confirmed victories, Colonel." Lilia responded. "And more than a thousand hours flight time before we joined," she continued.

"Yes, I can read," he replied. "You will start your training tomorrow."

"We don't need more training, Sir. We've come to fight." Katya said boldly.

"I see that you have some experience. But you've been sent to my regiment, and you're going to do things my way. I'm not putting you on the flight roster until I know you're ready for it." Baranov replied then stood. "Now come with me."

Baranov exited the bunker and brought Lilia and Katya toward the aircraft lineup, where Sasha and Aleksei were still standing.

"Sasha, Aleksei, these are Staff Sergeants Budanova, and Litvyak." The Colonel motioned to Aleksei. "Litvyak, you'll be training with Captain Solomatin. Budanova, you'll be flying with Captain Martinov, starting tomorrow. See the base field commander. He will show you to your quarters." The Colonel pointed to the field commander standing near a munitions crate. "That is all for now," he said, and walked back to the command bunker.

"We don't need training," Lilia said to Aleksei. "We've each got two victories already."

Aleksei took note of the two small red stars on her plane. He shrugged. It was only two, after all. It could have been luck. Every pilot knew that it took five stars to earn the title of Ace, and nobody got five stars on luck.

"I take my orders from the Colonel," Aleksei replied.

Lilia looked over Aleksei, still unsure what to make of him. Was it confidence, or arrogance? She couldn't yet tell.

"Alexander Martinov," Sasha introduced himself to Katya cordially.

"Katya Budanova," she replied.

"Tomorrow we'll see what you've got," said Sasha.

"Tomorrow it is." Katya responded. "Let's find our quarters, Lilia."

With the late winter afternoon quickly turning to darkness Lilia and Katya parted to find their bunks for the night. They were lead to a snow-covered bunker. The inside was sparse; a potbelly stove, two cots with wool blankets, and a small lantern. A tea kettle set atop the small stove. They later found the canteen and ate a hot meal of stew and black bread before settling in for their first winter night at the new regiment. Katya got a fire going inside the potbelly stove providing some warmth as the temperature outside quickly dropped.

Lying in their cots, under blankets, Katya dimmed the lantern. The bunker, lit only by the faint orange glow from the stove was the most peaceful place they had been in months. At the other bases there were always noises through the night, if only the faint rumbling of bombs going off somewhere.

"We can't let them keep us from the fight this time." Katya said. "I couldn't bear it. I want vengeance for my mother and my sister." she continued. Her hometown of Smolensk was still occupied by the Germans. "So we'll really show them what we've got tomorrow. Then we'll kick the fascists out of our country."

"It isn't just about beating the fascists for me," replied Lilia. "I love my country and I want to save it, but I want five stars to live in it." Katya listened curiously.

"No one can say my father was an enemy if his daughter is an ace," Lilia continued.

Katya paused before asking in a near breathless whisper, "The Purge?"

Lilia nodded. "You mustn't speak of it...to anyone." Katya said in a hushed voice.

Lilia nodded again. "You'll get your stars, Lilka." Katya said decisively.

The next morning, they were up before the sun. Fayina and her tool cart had arrived pre-dawn by truck. Lilia and Fayina greeted each other with a quick hug as if each trying to steal some warmth from the other in the frigid morning air. Lilia and Katya were both wrapped up in bulky winter flight suits, the cold only hitting their faces. Colonel Baranov approached, the steam rising from a mug of tea in his hand catching the first rays of the morning sun.

"That's the Colonel," Lilia said to Fayina.

"Fayina Pleshivtseva, reporting for duty," she said with a salute.

"Get these aircraft ready for flight," Baranov replied.

"Yes, Comrade Colonel," she answered back.

The radiators of their Yak fighters had been drained of water the night before to prevent them from freezing. The first task of each day at the new base was to boil large pots of water and fill them again.

Aleksei and Sasha found their trainees by the flight line as the aircraft were being prepared for flight.

"Good morning, Sergeant Litvyak," Aleksei said to Lilia.

"Good morning, Captain," she replied.

Fayina quickly finished her pre-flight check, and had the aircraft fueled.

"Ready for flight, Lilia," Fayina called out.

"When we get up there, just try to stay on my wing," Aleksei said, then walked to his airplane further down the line.

Lilia climbed into her airplane. She started the engine and was soon in the air, following Aleksei's airplane off the runway. After reaching altitude and leveling off, she put her airplane slightly back and to the right of Captain Solomatin.

"On your wing, Captain." Lilia called out over the radio.

"Stay on my wing, Seagull. Rolling left." He called out, then threw his aircraft into a tight left turn and rolled over in a corkscrew.

Lilia followed closely, holding position on a new heading.

"Breaking right." Aleksei called out, then pulled into a tight right turn and roll into a new heading and altitude.

Lilia followed closely again, holding his wing position. After this he called out several more rolls and turns. Each time she held position, but grew frustrated being asked to demonstrate maneuvers she had executed hundreds of times before.

The two Yaks finally leveled off and held a straight course. In the moment he paused before calling out a new maneuver Lilia broke off his wing in a series off snap rolls and made a tight turn to put her airplane behind and to his left.

"Where are you, Seagull?" he called over the radio.

She turned again and pushed her airplane to full throttle, putting their airplanes on a collision course from his 7 o'clock. At the last moment she climbed into a fast roll, putting her airplane directly above his, upside down, canopy to canopy.

"Right above you, Captain," Lilia called out. Aleksei looked up to see her in her cockpit above him only three meters away. Lilia completed the roll to his right side and fell back into wing position.

"On your wing, Captain," she called out again.

It was a daredevil move that only a highly skilled pilot could have pulled off with such precision, and he knew it. There could be no denying she had mastered the aircraft.

"Back to base," came Aleksei's curt response.

The two returned to base without further dialogue and taxied into the line up next to each other. Aleksei was standing next to Lilia's airplane when she stepped down from the wing.

"So how did I do?" Lilia asked.

"You disobeyed my direct orders," he replied sharply. "And that move you pulled was reckless."

"But I did pull it off," Lilia replied.

"This is not a place for stunt flying. It's not a game up there," said Aleksei as Lilia rolled her eyes. "Do you see those stars on my airplane?" Aleksei asked. Lilia looked toward his aircraft and all the small red stars painted on it. There were too many to count at a glance-more than a dozen. He was an Ace at least twice over. "They were all good pilots. Some of them were just reckless."

Lilia shrugged as Katya and Sasha taxied their airplanes into the line up. Sasha and Katya both stepped down from their wings to join Lilia and Aleksei, an obvious grin on Sasha's face.

"How did this one do?" Sasha called out to Aleksei, who merely shook his head in response as Colonel Baranov emerged from the command bunker.

"Sasha, Aleksei, come over!" Baranov yelled across the airfield, beckoning the two younger pilots. Sasha and Aleksei left to join the Colonel in the command bunker.

Lilia and Katya stood by their aircraft, waiting to learn their fate when Fayina joined them. She had been listening to Lilia's exchange with Aleksei as she blocked the wheels and pulled her tool cart toward the aircraft.

"How did you make him so angry, Lilia?" asked Fayina.

"Showed him I can fly, that's all," Lilia replied.

Inside the command bunker, Aleksei stood by Baranov's desk bemoaning Lilia's move.

"They need more training. How can we take them into a fight if they won't follow orders?" said Aleksei.

Baranov listened quietly, then turned to Sasha, seated by him with a wide grin on his face.

"What do you say, Sasha?" Baranov asked.

Sasha leaned in, smiling. "I tell you, Kolya, these girls can really fly," he said with enthusiasm.

Baranov stood up and put a hand on Aleksei's shoulder.

"I don't like the idea of putting women into combat any more than you," Baranov intoned. "But these are the pilots they've sent us, and they are qualified. You know that. They are a lot more qualified than some of the boys they've sent us before." Baranov walked toward the flight roster hanging on the wall near his desk. "They know the risks and they've come to fight. I'm putting them on the roster." Baranov said as he picked up a pen. "You are going to keep flying with Lityak, and Sasha will fly with Budanova. Those are my orders."

"This girl will be the end of me," Aleksei said in refrain.

For the time, the matter was settled. The names Litvyak and Budanova were added to the flight roster. They had found a home at the front, and for good or ill, at the 296th IAP they were to be treated as equals.

Chapter 6

Fayina Pleshivtseva pulled her tool cart across trampled snow and ice in the early morning through the lineup of fighter planes toward Lilia's airplane. As she passed the propeller she saw a male pilot staring curiously at the white lily painted on the fuselage, in awe at something that seemed so out of place in the midst of a war. Fayina pulled her cart to the nose of the plane then stopped to stare at the pilot. He was handsome, she thought, and taller than most of the other pilots, the rank of Lieutenant visible on his sleeve. Fayina stood still observing him as he stared at the insignia. A moment passed before he turned to notice her.

"Are you the artist that painted this?" he asked.

"Would you like me to paint some flowers on your plane, Lieutenant?" she replied.

He laughed out loud. "Maybe something a little more dangerous looking, a tiger, or maybe a lightning bolt," he said with a smile.

"Let me know when you decide and I'll get right to it," she offered.

"I will do that..." he replied.

"Fayina," she said.

"Pleased to meet you, Fayina," he replied. "Mikhail."

"Good luck up there today, Lieutenant Mikhail," she said.

"Thank you...Fayina," he replied.

They smiled at one another as he walked toward his airplane before Fayina went to work. It was just after dawn.

The other ground crew had been up before first light, boiling water to fill the radiators. They moved down the line up, filling the radiator of Lilia's fighter plane as Fayina was finishing the rest of her pre-flight checks. She dove head first into the cockpit, making sure the blocks on the pedals that Lilia needed to reach them were secure. She had cleaned the Perspex canopy with a clean cloth for maximum visibility, and tested the tension of aileron cables. Armorers and refueling crews moved down the line up as well, loading the fighter plane with its full carry of fuel and ammunition. Now that Lilia was on the flight roster, there was no predicting what she might encounter in the air.

By January of 1943, the German 6th Army had been encircled in a pocket in the City of Stalingrad, cut off from the rest of the German line. Hitler had refused General Paulus' request to break out of the Stalingrad pocket and re-establish lines of supply. The focus of the Luftwaffe was now to fly

Junkers Ju-52 transport planes into several small runways to resupply worn out and undersupplied German troops on the ground inside the city. Holding the pocket became the whole of Hitler's objective in Stalingrad.

Lilia and Aleksei walked out of the command bunker in winter flight gear, followed by Sasha Martinov and Katya Budanova across the snow toward the aircraft line up. Their orders were to intercept and deter the Ju-52 transport ships from dropping their supplies inside Stalingrad. Aleksei walked up to Lilia's aircraft, inspecting its wings. He checked the tension on the left aileron, pushing it smoothly up and down.

"What are you doing?" Lilia asked.

"Inspecting your airplane. I can't have you dropping out of a fight over mechanical issues." Aleksei responded.

"I have a mechanic who already does that." Lilia replied.

Fayina snapped to attention before Aleksei. "Captain, the airplane is fully fueled and armed," she said.

"And you've completed the full inspection yourself?" Aleksei asked.

"Yes, Captain, absolutely ready for flight." Fayina said confidently.

Aleksei nodded. "Good," he replied, and walked toward his own aircraft.

It was to be their first operational combat mission together. They had yet to develop a rapport. Lilia climbed onto the wing of her airplane and into the cockpit.

Ten minutes later, Lilia, Aleksei, Katya and Sasha were near the western edge of Stalingrad in a formation of four, two pairs that could split up in combat if necessary. They flew their patrol over Soviet held territory just outside the city between the pocket and the German line. In their first three sorties of the day, they encountered no enemy aircraft. They refueled again and took off on a fourth sortie of the day in the early afternoon. As they reached the western edge of Stalingrad, the call came over the radio. Spotters had seen a formation of four Junkers Ju-52 transports making a run for the pocket with Messerschmitt 109s flying high cover. Each Ju-52 had a four-person crew, one pilot and three gunners. There were two gunners in the waist position and one in the rear of the tri-motor transports-originally designed to be passenger airplanes.

Katya was first to spot the formation and called it out, coming in at 10 o'clock low. Aleksei, as flight commander, gave the order to gain altitude for a high frontal attack. There could be as many as twelve guns firing back, but the Ju-52's best defensive coverage was to the rear.

"Increase speed, dive, and engage." Aleksei called out.

The four Yak formation quickly gained speed. Closing fast, they opened up gun bursts, blasting rounds at the Ju-52's front ends. Lilia connected with a Ju-52's right engine, setting it on fire. The Ju-52s scattered in all directions, breaking formation, their gunners firing wildly. Two Messerschmitt 109 fighters quickly jumped into the fight, diving and firing on the Yaks.

"Split formation." Aleksei called out.

The Ju-52s had already turned to run as the Messerschmitts appeared. Aleksei and Lilia turned to fight off one Messerschmitt, while Katya and Sasha turned to handle the other. Outnumbered and already having failed their primary mission, the Messerschmitts quickly dove away and ran. The Ju-52s, though much slower than the Yak-1, quickly made it back across the German line, with two trailing smoke from their burning engines. The four Yaks turned back to avoid the anti-aircraft cannons they would encounter if they got too close to the German line at low altitude.

After spending half of their ammunition on the initial pass at the Ju-52s, Aleksei gave the order to return to base. While they scattered the transports and briefly tangled with the fighter escort, they hadn't downed any aircraft, yet they had succeeded in their mission of blocking supplies from reaching German troops inside Stalingrad.

As Lilia and Aleksei pulled into the line-up, Fayina blocked the wheels on Lilia's airplane. Lilia quickly climbed down from the wing to join Aleksei. While Fayina assessed the airplane she could see that any grudge or misgiving Lilia might have had with Aleksei seemed to have vanished. She overheard only bits of their conversation as they headed toward the command bunker to file their reports, "…inflection point… moment of engagement." They spoke the academics of air combat, and it wasn't Fayina's job to know these things. It was her job to keep the aircraft ready for flight, which was demanding enough in frozen conditions. Bolts would freeze in place, coolant lines and fuel lines would crack.

By the afternoon, another brutal winter storm was moving in quickly. Orders had already been given to suspend all further flights. It was time to get the radiators drained, and cover the airplanes in tarps for the night. Flurries of snow from the approaching storm had started to blow across the airfield. In mid-January, the days were short and the nights were long. Fayina chose to keep working. It was easier to make certain adjustments when the engine was still warm and there was daylight, than it was in the dark early hours when the machine would be frozen again. Fayina worked quickly as the sunlight faded.

The Chief Mechanic was soon barking orders down the line. "Get the radiators drained before they freeze! Quickly, we've got a storm coming." He yelled.

Fayina had gotten the radiator drained but struggled to replace the drain plug on Lilia's fighter, her fingers freezing to the metal bolt. In mere moments, the winds were blowing snow across the airfield and through the line up. A male mechanic passed by, covering himself in a long coat and hood.

"Leave it, Fayina. That's enough for today. Get to the shelter," he said and then was out of sight.

Fayina continued, struggling against the wind to cover the airplane in tarps, tying them down to the wheels. As she finished, covering her tool cart under the airplane's wing, the snow had cut her visibility to only a few feet. The whiteout turned to grey as the light dimmed further. Fayina walked in the direction she thought was toward the shelter, though it wouldn't stand out, being only a few wooden boards propped up to keep the snow off.

"Hello?" Fayina called out, hoping for a response that might give her for some sense of direction. "Anyone?" she called out again. She must be somewhere between the line up and the shelter, she thought. There were no lights in any direction. If she was past the shelter and the bunker and kept going she might be lost completely. Suddenly a figure appeared beside her and took her by the arm. She could make out only the outline of a mask and goggles.

"This way." he spoke, leading her in the darkness.

Further on there was a door. It opened and a dim sliver of light appeared. She followed the goggled figure inside and closed the door behind her. The small bunker was lit only by small flames inside a potbelly stove. A match was struck and a lamp appeared. Fayina stood quietly as the figure took off his mask and goggles. It was Mikhail, the pilot she had met early that morning.

"It's you…" she said, partially to herself.

Mikhail pointed to the potbelly stove. "Get yourself warm," he said.

Fayina moved across the bunker and huddled by the stove nervously, holding out her numb fingers.

"I don't think I'm supposed to be in here. Isn't it against regulations?" she asked.

"There's a blizzard out there. You could freeze to death." He replied. "Besides, it isn't right to have women sleeping outside in winter."

Fayina studied him nervously, warming herself by the stove as he prepared a pot of tea. "All the mechanics are sleeping outside. I'm a mechanic. I only ask to be treated equally to the other mechanics," she answered.

"Was chivalry defeated in the revolution?" he asked, then passed her a cup. He lifted the tea kettle from the small stove and filled the cup.

"Thank you." She said, feeling her fingers again.

They stood together by the stove drinking tea as the wind whistled outside the door. Mikhail then found a bedroll and an extra blanket, laying it down for her next to the stove. "Stay here, at least until the storm passes," he said.

The wind soon ceased making noise, giving way to a different kind of silence as the snow laid a cocoon over the bunker. Fayina lay down on the bedroll. As Mikhail moved to turn down the lamp, he stopped quickly, his face wincing from a sharp pain.

Fayina caught his expression. "You're injured?" she asked, then sat up.

"It's nothing," he replied. "I was nicked by a tail gunner."

"Let me see it."

Mikhail sat on the edge of the cot and pulled back his shirt to reveal a poorly bandaged wound below his right shoulder, as though it was a mark of shame.

"I can do better than that," Fayina said, then paused. "Did you bandage this yourself?" She asked.

"It's nothing." He replied.

"It's a bullet wound. That isn't nothing. Where is the medical kit?"

Mikhail pointed next to the stove, reluctantly. Fayina picked up the small canvas pouch and opened it to find a small brown bottle of iodine, alcohol, and a fresh bandage. She sat next to him on the cot and reached to remove the old bandage. Fayina inspected the old bandage on his arm, tugging at a loose end to remove it. Mikhail winced again in pain, pulling away with a grunt. Fayina stopped.

"Nothing?" she repeated his words. "Big tough guy, huh?"

He offered up his arm again. Fayina went back to work, gently, trying not to arouse pain as she unwrapped the old bandage.

"Are you afraid when you're up there?" Fayina asked, attempting to take his mind off of the wound.

"Everyone is, but you don't think of it." He replied.

"How many planes have you shot down?" she asked.

"Three," he answered. "It's just a number. If there ever was such a thing as honor or glory in a war, there won't be much room for it in this one, not for us at least. The best we can hope for is to survive and not disappoint our fellow soldiers."

Fayina cleaned the small wound on his arm. It looked as though a bullet had grazed it just below the shoulder and taken an inch long mark of skin and flesh. Fayina tried to be quick but gentle, as Mikhail held back the pain.

"Then why fighters?" Fayina asked, distracting him again.

"In a time of crisis, every man must go where he is needed most." He replied then paused for a moment. "They say that men are made by the times in which they live. I shouldn't expect my fate to be any different."

"Be still." Fayina said as she applied fresh iodine to the wound.

Mikhail gritted his teeth and pushed a clenched fist to his knee. Fayina finished, then pulled out a fresh bandage to wrap his arm. As she wrapped his arm, he couldn't help but study her face as she worked, learning its features from the dim light of the oil lamp and the orange glow from the stove. Fayina tied off the bandage, now neatly wrapped around his upper right arm.

"That should do," she said as she finished, looking up to catch him staring at her.

"Thank you," he said softly.

Fayina stood up and turned down the lamp.

"You need rest."

Mikhail lay back on the cot. Fayina lay down on the bedroll and covered herself in the blanket. In the dim orange light of the stove and the warmth of the bunker, she watched Mikhail close his eyes and sleep for almost half an hour before drifting off to sleep herself. It would be her most restful sleep in months.

Two days later the storm had broken, and so had the will of the German 6th Army. The airlift had failed in its mission to re-supply the German troops inside Stalingrad. Three more days of snow and frigid cold without enough proper winter clothing had pushed them past the breaking point. News of the surrender reached the airfield mid-morning while ground crews were still digging the planes out from under fresh fallen snow, preparing to get back into the fight.

Colonel Baranov stepped out of the command bunker and approached the line up with a wide grin. Seeing his smile was enough to cause every pilot, mechanic, armorer, and ground crew to stop what they were doing and wait for his booming voice to deliver some announcement. None could remember the last time they had seen the Colonel smile, if they had seen such a thing at all.

"There will be no flights today." He said to great anticipation. "General Paulus has surrendered! The battle for Stalingrad has been won!"

Lilia and Aleksei were standing by their aircraft when Baranov made the announcement. Several pilots pulled out their pistols and fired in the air, yelling further down the line.

"The battle for Stalingrad has been won! General Paulus has surrendered!" one shouted, only to hear it repeated down the line up. More shots rang out. Lilia and Aleksei turned to each other smiling in reserved celebration, then hugged each other as cheers broke out across the snow-covered airfield.

Colonel Baranov then ordered all personnel to spend the morning washing and repairing their uniforms, and to bath before a medals ceremony in the afternoon. The luxury of hot water, soap, and clean clothing gave a welcome break to the past months of fighting day in and day out with little regard to such things. It was a chance to wash away the grime and the feeling of constant stress, a collective exhale. It was a rare gift, a day away from the fight if only for a day. By the afternoon, the entire regiment was dressed in their best uniforms.

Colonel Baranov had the entire regiment lined up in rows, standing over fresh snow in the crisp air. He read out several proclamations of gratitude and congratulations from the high command, then issued shiny medals and personally pinned them to uniforms. A photographer had been sent to document the ceremony. He found Lilia and Aleksei next to their aircraft.

"Could I get a photograph, Sergeant Litvyak?" He asked.

Aleksei nudged her forward. "Give them a nice picture, Lilia. Let the people know who fights for them," he said, eliciting a smile from her.

"Could you stand on the wing, please?" the photographer asked. Lilia obliged and climbed onto the wing of her fighter plane as the photographer set up a tripod to compose his shot. "Now, look in that direction." He said, pointing toward the nose of the airplane.

Lilia turned her head toward the horizon, a subtle wind catching her hair as the photographer took the shot of her, in profile, on the wing of her aircraft. "Thank you, Sergeant Litvyak," he said, picking up his camera.

Celebrations commenced in the evening after supper was served. The pilots and officers gathered in the command bunker, quickly transforming it into a raucous party with everyone singing patriotic songs set to the balalaika. Shots of vodka were poured all around and toasts were made.

"To beating the fascist invaders in the battle for Stalingrad!" a pilot shouted, and the pilots downed a shot.

Lilia passed her shot of vodka to Aleksei. "You take it."

"I thought you were from Moscow. You don't like vodka? I thought all Muscovites loved vodka." He replied.

"Where are you from?" She asked.

Aleksei took the shot glass and held it up to drink to his hometown, "Kaluga!" he said, and downed the shot.

"A country boy. Yes, I can see it in you." Lilia prodded amidst the singing. "Any brothers or sisters?"

"I have a sister." Aleksei replied. "And you?"

"Little brother, Yuri." She answered.

Across the bunker sat Mikhail, quietly, watching the proceedings. While the others were distracted by toasts and singing Mikhail found his overcoat and snuck out of the bunker. Several more rounds of toasts followed, and Colonel Baranov ordered the vodka rations doubled. After several more songs and toasts, he ordered them tripled.

Mikhail could hear the command bunker erupt in another round of singing as he walked across the airbase. There were pockets of celebration all over. He passed a group of armorers sitting around an open fire to stay warm, singing with mugs of hot tea. He walked further, past the rows of aircraft, as the noise of another celebration grew louder. It was the sound of ground crews and mechanics in the aircraft repair shop. He stood by the door and looked in to see them amongst the wrenches and tools and an airplane engine in pieces. They were all clapping, stomping their feet, and some dancing like Cossacks while belting out a patriotic song, *The Sacred War* "… arise for a fight to the death, against the dark fascist forces, against the cursed hordes…"

Fayina stood in a corner, clapping along to the beat. Mikhail spotted her and snuck in just enough to show her his face. She met his eyes and he nodded for her come over. In a moment, she had found her coat and slipped out of the shop to meet him on the frozen ground.

"Shouldn't you be in the command bunker?" Fayina asked.

"I wanted to find you." Mikhail replied.

Fayina smiled at him. They stood face to face, now in clean uniforms. The night was quiet again without the distant rumble of bombs, gunfire and Katyusha rockets. They both listened to the silence for a moment as Fayina had suddenly noticed it. She had kept her head down in the work of keeping the airplane ready for flight for months, always some detail to attend. In the midst of it all, she hadn't the time to reflect on what it all meant. It hit her just then, the scope and scale of what they had been a part. It was the largest and most technologically advanced battle in the history of the world and they had each played their part in winning it. The silence of the night was proof. If it wasn't the time to celebrate, there could never be a time to celebrate anything. They moved closer and suddenly kissed. Mikhail took her hand and they walked to his bunker. While the rest of the regiment danced and sang, and drank vodka, Fayina and Mikhail found celebration in each other's arms.

"I'm going to call you Ina... Ina, my angel of Stalingrad." He said, stroking her sandy blonde hair. "Ina..."

Chapter 7

In recognition for their contribution to winning the battle of Stalingrad, the 296th IAP was re-designated as an elite Guards unit, to become the 73rd GIAP. Baranov read out the proclamation in a brief ceremony in the early afternoon the day after their celebration of victory. After a day of rest, the airfield returned to its usual rhythm, and the war continued.

Of the 400,000 German troops that had marched into Stalingrad, 90,000 would march out as prisoners of war. Only 6,000 would ever see Germany again. Total loss of human life on both sides was close to a million people, and the war was far from over. After the Stalingrad pocket was cleared, tactics would change. The front was now a nearly 3,000 kilometer line that was ever-changing over varied terrain. The Soviet Air Defense operated various layers of air cover, ground attack bombers at the lowest elevation, bombers above them, and fighters, and fighter escorts higher still. Lilia and Aleksei were also given a re-designation of duties. For the time, they were given the title of Free Hunters. Their missions were to seek out targets of opportunity at any elevation, to search and destroy.

Colonel Baranov had also given the order to get all airplanes and equipment assessed and repaired. The pilots of the regiment would spend the rest of the day in the command bunker studying maps of the frontline and determining tactics to use in destroying enemy targets. Their new duties would include all possible types of air and ground engagement, including fixed targets, railway junctions, and supply columns. Since the Battle of Stalingrad had been won, it was time for the newly designated 73rd Guards to join the wider war on the frontline.

Lilia and Aleksei prepared for their first patrol together as Free Hunters only days after the battle of Stalingrad had been won. As they strapped into their parachute harnesses, Lilia looked at Aleksei, studying his mood.

"We took back Stalingrad. Now we take Berlin. Are you ready, Kaluga?" She asked.

"Perhaps we should just work on our sector for now," he answered.

Aleksei smiled and at the same time marveled at her, realizing she was the most interesting person he had ever known. What might their meeting have amounted to had it occurred under different circumstances? He had come to respect and trust in her skills as a pilot. In only a month she had become vital to his very survival. He hadn't felt as close to many people in his life, and in the past three years of the war had come to believe it was better not to become too close to anyone.

Fresh from their victory in the Battle of Stalingrad, Colonel Baranov had granted Katya Budanova's request to visit her sister in Moscow. Mid-morning on the 11th of February, Lilia and Aleksei stood by the flight line with Colonel Baranov and Sasha Martinov when the alert came over the radio in panicked voices. A formation of more than 26 enemy aircraft had been spotted inbound for the front line. The news was shouted down the flight line.

"We're back to the fight. Stay on my wing." Aleksei said as he rushed toward his airplane.

Lilia strapped on her flight helmet and climbed into her cockpit.

"Sasha, you'll fly my wing," Baranov called out, strapping on his own flight helmet as he rushed to a Yak-1 fighter.

The four Yak fighter planes sped along the runway and were quickly in the air as a formation of four, racing to the frontline at near full throttle. Lilia was first to spot the formation of enemy aircraft, appearing like a cluster of black birds in the distance, and called it out.

Soviet troops had dug in, attempting to hold the line, as the Luftwaffe tried to break their will from above. A formation of Junkers 87 dive-bombers had reached the front line and chosen their targets on the ground. Soldiers of the Red Army hunkered down helpless in a trench, clutching their rifles in anticipation of the terrifying screech of death from above, for which they had nowhere to hide and no means to defend themselves. Nothing else could make a soldier on the ground feel more helpless and exposed.

Hugging the bottom of the trench, soldiers turned their faces to the sky in terror as the screeching wail of a JU-87 erupted. The aircraft dove straight at them, ready to release its bomb. The screeching continued on as several soldiers cried out in terror. The airplane came closer still, the screeching louder, almost close enough to make out the face of the pilot. Bullets suddenly ripped across the sky, punching hot lead into the fuselage. A single bullet hit the bomb on its undercarriage, destroying the dive-bomber in a massive explosion. The soldiers in the trench were at first shocked as flaming wreckage fell to the ground twenty meters away, then a moment later Lilia's fighter plane roared across the sky above them. They stood and cheered, pumping their rifles in the air.

Baranov had ordered the formation split into pairs to scatter the formation of Stukas. Seeing the first bomber explode mid-air, the others quickly broke off their attack and scattered to escape back across the line. Lilia and Aleksei moved back into wing position and banked hard left to set aim on a fleeing bomber. Aleksei spotted the fighter escort above them and called it out.

"Fighters! Six o'clock, high." Lilia heard over the radio.

Two Focke-Wulf 190s moved in just after the Stukas began to scatter. The intent of their combined mission was to force a break in the Red Army line so their troops on the ground could exploit it. The Stukas had failed and already fled, yet the Focke-Wulfs engaged in the fight without them. Across the wider frontline, the war would be won or lost in the battle for air superiority, which would be settled by the fighter squadrons and the skills of their pilots on both sides of the line.

The Focke-Wulfs first pass would come in the form of a high-speed diving attack. Aleksei had seen this tactic many times before. They would use their altitude advantage to make their kill in one pass and if the tactic failed, the pilots could then use their speed to get away.

"Stay close on my wing and be ready to break high right." Aleksei said calmly.

The Focke-Wulfs fired their first volley of bullets, streaking past the two Yaks. Mere seconds passed as the Focke-Wulfs continued gaining speed until they were fully committed to their line of attack. At that moment Aleksei called out.

"Now!" He told her.

Lilia stayed tight on Aleksei's wing position as he pulled hard up and to the right, up and over as the Focke-Wulfs screamed past them, then down into a corkscrew and behind the two diving German fighters at full throttle. The Focke-Wulfs quickly reached such low altitude; they had no choice but to pull out of their dive. Their airspeed slowed as they pulled up and became larger targets in Aleksei's gun sights. He fired off cannon rounds, the fourth round hitting the lead fighters engine, sending black smoke streaming from the fuselage. The damaged enemy plane banked hard right, away from his wingman and out of the fight.

Lilia and Aleksei stayed on the tail of the remaining Focke-Wulf, still gaining speed. They soon caught up to the lone pilot, dropping airspeed to stay behind him and line up the shot. The pilot pulled hard left attempting to evade the two Yak fighters behind him.

"He's breaking left!" Aleksei called out. "Take my left wing."

As the German pilot made a series of zig-zags, Lilia bounced to Aleksei's left rear position, both firing short bursts, stitching bullets into the remaining Focke-Wulf, Lilia taking advantage of the wider angle.

"Breaking right!" Aleksei called out again.

Lilia bounced to Aleksei's right rear position and let out another burst, clipping rounds into the Focke-Wulf's tail section. Aleksei fired another burst, tearing up the enemy fighter's left wing.

Lilia's final burst set the fighters engine on fire, sending out a trail of smoke.

"Got him!" Lilia called out.

The soldiers on the ground had watched the entire battle, their eyes fixed on the sky above as the airplanes tangled in trails of smoke and bullets. As Lilia crossed back across the frontline, she looked down to see the men cheering, pumping their fists and rifles in the air in gratitude to the pilot who had likely saved their lives. As she made a low pass, waggling her wings in acknowledgement, none of them knew their champion knight on wings was a woman.

Colonel Baranov called the order over the radio to fall back in formation and return to base. Lilia climbed back onto Aleksei's wing position as they turned east.

"Stay on my wing. We need some altitude." Aleksei called out over the radio.

The pair throttled up and gained altitude through layers of scattered clouds. As Aleksei pulled through the top layer of clouds he checked his wing position to find that Lilia was nowhere in sight.

"Seagull, where are you?" He called over the radio.

Aleksei pulled the stick to circle around for another view, thinking she must be lost somewhere in the clouds below.

"Seagull Ninety, respond." Aleksei called out again, frantically searching the sky for any sight of her airplane. He circled again, looking above and below. "Seagull Ninety, respond." He called out again. "Where are you?" No response was returned over the headset. Aleksei looked at his fuel gauge, then circled once more. Lilia still nowhere in sight, he returned to base alone.

When Aleksei landed at the airfield, Colonel Baranov and Sasha Martinov were already out of their aircraft and standing by the lineup. Aleksei pulled his fighter plane into the lineup, hoping Lilia would already be there, while noticing her absence. The aircrew put blocks under the wheels and Aleksei climbed down from the cockpit to join Sasha and Colonel Baranov.

"Where is Litvyak?" The Colonel asked sharply.

"We were separated in the cloud layer." Aleksei answered, looking nervously at the sky. "She should have been back by now. She'll be out of fuel soon." Aleksei lamented, the worry obvious in his voice.

They all stood together, watching the sky. The airfield seemed to go silent, and with each passing minute their doubts of Lilia's return would only grow.

As another minute ticked by, even the Colonel began to fear the worst, yet held his breath. Ina observed the scene, standing next to her tool cart and the empty slot where Lilia's aircraft should have been. Ina too, began to hold her breath. A moment later, somewhere in the distance came the rumbling of the Klimov engine, growing louder.

"There she is!" Aleksei called out, suddenly relieved.

A second later Lilia's aircraft roared over the airfield, upside down.

"Doing stunts over my airfield!" Baranov shouted angrily, turning to see Aleksei with a grin on his face.

"You approve is this hooliganism?" Baranov asked.

"She's celebrating another victory." Aleksei answered. "She blew up a Stuka."

"She should be flying a broomstick!" Baranov countered.

Sasha stood next to them laughing out loud as Lilia snap rolled and pulled up into a full loop. Baranov looked on, shaking his head. Lilia finished the loop and banked hard left, flying low over their heads to test their nerves. Sasha ducked as she flew over them and laughed even harder. Lilia then turned again and touched down with an even glide.

"Look at that landing!" Sasha called out, pointing to the fighter plane with the lily painted on its fuselage.

Colonel Baranov finally lost his restraint and let out a deep belly laugh.

"This magnificent little devil they've sent us!" Baranov exclaimed.

Lilia's aircraft bounced along the runway and taxied into the lineup next to them.

Fayina had been standing back watching the entire show when Baranov called out to her. "Paint another star on the plane, Fayina!"

The Focke-Wulf 190 had been a shared victory with Aleksei, but the Stuka she had shot down would count as her third star. Lilia climbed down from the wing of her plane to join the other pilots with a smile.

"To the command bunker!" Baranov said in his booming voice. "Let us write the reports."

Lilia headed toward the command bunker with Colonel Baranov and Sasha Martinov. Aleksei hesitated for a moment as he watched her. The elation suddenly drained from his face, giving way to a new realization. In a matter of only minutes he had gone from terrifying worry to overwhelming joy. It was then that he knew the love he felt for Lilia was real. It sat like a stone in his stomach. He had feared it for a time, but now there was no use denying it. He could not hide in a cloak of cynicism from himself. Aleksei pondered the thought a moment and then followed the other pilots toward the command bunker.

Lilia and Aleksei sat together for supper in the canteen, a meal of black bread and stew. Lilia's third star had given her a new confidence she hadn't previously known. She talked excitedly about the day's events. Aleksei nodded in agreement and smiled. It was odd, she thought. Their situation had somehow reversed. She was usually the quiet one, while Aleksei went into exhaustive discussions of strategies and tactics, especially after an eventful day. After the meal, Lilia traded her one hundred gram vodka ration to Sasha for his one hundred gram chocolate ration. She kept a curious eye on Aleksei, still wondering what had caused the change in his demeanor. Lilia watched as he stood up and gathered his coat and turned to leave the bunker.

Aleksei walked outside the bunker, the winter air still crisp, snow crunching underfoot, contemplating the weight of his situation. The night had grown dark and the war had temporarily become quiet again. Lilia appeared at the bunker door, wrapping herself in her winter coat to follow him.

"Hey, Kaluga. Wait up." Lilia called after him.

Aleksei stopped and turned to face her.

"You barely said two words to me at supper, " she continued. "You don't seem yourself all of a sudden."

"I'm not, and I doubt I ever will be again." Aleksei answered.

She stared at him quizzically a moment, then asked "What do you mean?"

"I have a problem," he answered.

"What is it?" She replied

Aleksei shrugged, not finding the words, and knowing that if he did find them there could be no taking them back.

Lilia pushed him for an answer. "Come on, Kaluga. Tell me."

Aleksei smiled back at her thinking, she was the light and she was life, and all that was worth fighting for and protecting. She had altered the very nature and purpose of his existence. If there was a reason he should not divulge his feelings for her, he could not think of it at the moment. So he let the words out.

"I realized today that I love you," he said honestly.

Lilia took a step back to consider what it meant. She had not anticipated it as a possible answer. "What about the war, our duties?" she asked.

"We have each other up there. I'll protect you, and you'll protect me." Aleksei replied.

"I had thought perhaps we'd finish the fighting first, and then we'd both find love." Lilia answered.

"It's not our lot in life to plan far off tomorrows, Lilia." He replied. "The lives we live are right in front of us, here and now." Lilia took a step forward, thinking about it. "Besides, nobody finds love." Aleksei continued. "It has to find you."

"Did you just make that up?" She asked.

"No, old wives say it all the time." He answered.

"They do?"

Aleksei leaned towards her to speak in his most serious voice. "Lilia, I promise you, somewhere on this planet there is an old wife saying it right now."

Lilia burst out laughing, and then she kissed him.

Chapter 8

The surrender of the German 6th Army at Stalingrad had freed dozens of Red Army units to rejoin the Eastern Front. The reinforced line quickly put the German Army into retreat. It was during this time that Lilia had downed the Stuka to earn her third star. By the middle of February, the Red Army had retaken the southern city of Rostov-on-Don. A week later the 73rd Guards Regiment moved to a new airbase on the outskirts of the city by the Don River, near the Sea of Azov.

On the 23rd of February, 1943, at a solemn ceremony at the new airbase, both Lilia Litvyak and Katya Budanova were awarded the rank of Junior Lieutenant and issued the Order of the Red Star for their contributions to the victory in the battle for Stalingrad.

In the following weeks the German Army continued its systematic and strategic retreat. The Wehrmacht pulled back twenty-one divisions to reorganize and shorten their frontline. All the while, spring approached and the snow began to melt. The Red Army trudged through the muck of melting snow to reclaim town after town, each left in ruins, bridges destroyed, major roads and chokepoints cluttered with land mines. Lilia and Aleksei's missions over this time consisted of bomber escort, and ground support. The change of tides provided a relative calm in the air war. The changing season was also a welcome relief, offering a breath of warm air in the afternoon after a bitterly cold winter.

Lilia's relationship with Aleksei also blossomed. They had grown closer, flying missions by day, and a secret rendezvous at night. Their relationship had aroused suspicion and speculation at first, after which it became an open if still closely guarded secret amongst their fellow pilots and ground crew. To see them together, laughing and smiling, gave the entire regiment some measure of hope that something resembling normal life was still possible and would return again for all when the war was over.

Fayina and Mikhail had also kept up their meetings, although they both made every effort to hold it sacred and secret. They didn't dare show such obvious affection for each other as Lilia and Aleksei might on occasion. Fayina would wait until after supper, when the ground crews where laid in for the night before sneaking away to Mikhail's bunker. He would recite poetry and talk of his two sisters back home. Fayina had managed to keep it from Lilia for several weeks. When passing them near the canteen one evening, Lilia overheard a tiny parcel of conversation between them, less than half a sentence. More important was the tone of his voice, "...until then, Ina," said Mikhail in a whisper. Lilia said nothing about it for several days. She simply observed her mechanic doing her job, always cheerful despite the war. As Fayina finished cleaning the canopy of the fighter plane, Lilia waited for her to step down from the wing.

"Everything is ready, Lilia." Fayina said.

Lilia stepped up to climb into the cockpit, then turned. "Thank you, Ina." Lilia said quietly. Fayina froze and Lilia caught her stare. "Don't worry. Your secret is safe with me." Lilia whispered.

"Yours too," Fayina replied, before they both laughed out loud.

If Colonel Baranov had objections to any personal relationships, he kept them to himself. After all, he had been the one who had paired Lilia and Aleksei together in the first place. There was also the thought that the more they cared for each other, the harder they would fight for the sake of it. His mind was mostly occupied by the war. While the German Army had been in retreat, he knew the Luftwaffe had gained valuable time to repair and rebuild their fleet in preparation for a counter-offensive. It felt to him that the skies had been simply too calm for too long. Aleksei found the Colonel one evening before dusk, after a full day of ground support flights, watching the sky with a grim look on his face.

"What is it, Kolya?" Aleksei asked of Colonel Baranov, observing his expression.

"Something big is coming." The Colonel replied ominously. "We must be ready for it."

The German Army had gained most of its successes in the war to date by using the tactic of blitzkrieg, the lightning war, massive surprise attacks with overwhelming numbers. On the second day of spring, March the 22nd, of 1943, Colonel Baranov's prediction was proven true. The German Army had made their retreat to shorten and strengthen their own front-line, while the Luftwaffe prepared to re-engage in the air war. Their forces had gathered for the next blitz. The frantic calls came over the radio, reporting dozens of inbound bombers and fighters. Colonel Baranov wasted no time ordering all available planes and pilots into the air.

"Everyone up!" shouted the Colonel.

The pilots in readiness one at the end of the runway started their engines and took off immediately. Another pair of Yaks taxied to the end of the runway and quickly followed.

Lilia and Aleksei jumped in their cockpits and took off toward the front line. Turning on their radios, the airwaves were alive with chatter.

"Three dozen bombers reported, with fighter escort!" An unknown voice crackled through the radio. Coordinates from ground units followed. "Formation incoming northwest of the city, ninety kilometers."

"Changing course. Stay on my wing, Seagull," said Aleksei, veering right.

At their combined speed, on the correct course, they would meet the German bombers in a matter of minutes. Aleksei was first to spot the formation below them behind scattered clouds, two-dozen Junckers 88 bombers. Lilia was first to attack.

"I'm going in," she called out over the radio, pushing the throttle forward.

Lilia dove in on a single JU-88 in the rear of the formation. In a fast approach, she pressed the gun button, sending a streak of bullets into its left engine. Fire and black smoke streamed across the sky. She cut back the throttle, pulled the stick back and over to hit the crippled bomber's right engine. Several short burst from her guns quickly set it on fire.

Aleksei and Colonel Baranov had each targeted a single bomber, setting engines on fire, sending streams of white and black smoke. Injured bombers peeled out of formation, diving away. The result was chaotic as the entire formation began to scatter.

As Lilia moved into position to take down another bomber, she felt a sharp sting in her right leg. A bullet had pierced her cockpit. The pain was suddenly so intense she didn't notice the tears rolling down her face.

"One on your tail!" Aleksei's voice called over the radio. "Seagull!"

Lilia checked her mirrors to see a Messerschmitt 109 bobbing up and down behind her, trying to line her up in his sights.

"Break left!" Aleksei called out.

Lilia pulled hard on the stick, banking a hard left turn, ignoring the pain. Bullets streaked across the sky as Aleksei put the Messer in his sights, its fuselage exploding in a bright orange fireball.

"More in front of you!" Aleksei called out again.

Lilia looked ahead to see three more Messerschmitt 109s in a row, flying directly at her. Their noses lit up as they fired, their bullets streaking past her canopy on either side. Turning away and exposing herself as a larger target would be certain death. Her only chance was to hold the course and not lose her nerve. On a head to head collision course, the gap was closing fast, 400 meters, 300... 200... The German pilots' nerves broke first. They pulled away, fanning out in front of her. The middle fighter pulled up, exposing its light blue underbelly and black crosses. Lilia let out a steady burst of gunfire, ripping bullets into it. It's engine streaming black smoke, the Messer turned over and dove away in flames. All of the remaining German bombers and fighters had already scattered to the west.

"Seagull, take my wing." Aleksei said over the radio, suddenly appearing by Lilia's left wing. "It's over. Back to base." Aleksei continued.

Lilia did not respond, suddenly noticing the full measure of pain from her leg, and her adrenaline surging.

"Close call back there." Aleksei continued after a moment.

Lilia looked down to see the right leg of her flight suit soaked in blood.

"Seagull, respond."

"I'm hit." Lilia answered, tears returning to her face.

"Where?" Aleksei asked.

"In the leg." Lilia replied.

"Hold steady on my wing. We'll get you down." Aleksei assured her. Their base was still at least ten minutes away. "Keep talking to me, Seagull. Stay alert."

The wound was serious enough that Lilia could spill enough blood to lose consciousness. "Still here." Lilia answered.

Lilia stayed on Aleksei's wing, while fighting to stay conscious, and at the same time ignored the pain for several minutes.

"Seagull, switch to reserve fuel tank." Aleksei instructed.

"Switching tanks." Lilia replied, turning the switch in her cockpit.

"Slowing airspeed." Aleksei called out as he throttled back.

"Matching airspeed." Lilia responded, pulling back her throttle.

"Extend flaps." Aleksei called out.

"Extending flaps." Lilia responded, rotating the wheel in her cockpit.

"We're almost there. Put down your landing gear." Aleksei instructed next.

Lilia reached down to her right side to turn the knob to unlock her landing gear, felt a sharp sting, and let out a yell in response.

"Seagull!?"

"I can't reach it." Lilia replied.

Aleksei paused a moment, assessing the situation. "Leave them up and locked. We've got to get you down." Aleksei instructed as they approached the base.

"Leaving them up." Lilia acknowledged.

"Throttle back and put it down as slowly as you can."

Seeing the airbase runway a short distance away, Lilia pulled back the throttle to put the fighter plane nearly on a glide path, the propeller slowing its spin.

Ground crews watched as Lilia's airplane crossed the edge of the runway ten meters from the ground with no landing gear extended.

"Put it down." Aleksei said calmly.

Lilia's Yak touched down with a thud, the propeller digging in the dirt, sending the airplane into a sideways skid across the runway. Aleksei watched from the air as Lilia's airplane finally came to a stop. He circled back and landed a short distance further down the runway. Aleksei quickly jumped out of his airplane, climbed down from the wing and ran to Lilia's airplane, its wings laying flat on the runway. He stood on the left wing and pulled back her canopy to find Lilia unconscious.

"Lilia!" Ground crew arrived as Aleksei was unfastening her seat belt and harness. "Come on, Lilia. We've got to get you out of here."

She opened her eyes slightly at the sound of his voice.

"Stay with me." Aleksei said, reaching into the cockpit to lift her out.

Holding her in his arms, Aleksei noticed the Ground Crew gathered around him. "Get the doctor!" He shouted to them.

Aleksei carried Lilia in his arms as the ground crew ran for the airbase medic.

"Stay awake, Lilia. Stay with me."

Lilia passed in and out of consciousness, opening her eyes to see only the silhouette of Aleksei's worried face, against the clouds hanging in the blue sky above.

The airbase medic ran toward them with two of his staff carrying a stretcher. They reached Aleksei by the edge of the runway.

"Lay her down, please," instructed the medic.

Aleksei laid Lilia gently down on the stretcher. The medic checked her pulse and began to assess the wound to her leg, as various ground crew looked on worriedly, Fayina amongst them.

Colonel Baranov landed a minute later, next to Lilia's Yak-laying on its belly in the middle of the runway. He climbed out of his cockpit to observe the commotion, and Lilia on a stretcher.

"I can wrap the wound, but she'll have to go to the field hospital to get the metal taken out." The medic announced.

"Get the ambulance!" Baranov called out.

The medic wrapped fresh gauze tightly around Lilia's right leg while the ambulance was brought to the side of the runway.

"Aleksei, you go with her." Said the Colonel.

The medical staffers loaded Lilia into the back of the ambulance and Aleksei climbed in next to her.

Colonel Baranov had foreseen the attack, but it was Lilia's initiative and skill that had tipped the scales to scatter the formation and thwart the blitz. He called out to her just before the back doors of the ambulance were closed.

"You will have the title of Hero, Lilia. I promise you." The Colonel said in his booming voice.

The ambulance bumped along a dirt road at a decent rate of speed, jarring Lilia to open her eyes again to see Aleksei next to her. "Where are we going?" she asked.

"To a field hospital." Aleksei told her.

Lilia gritted her teeth as the pain suddenly returned to remind her of the day's events.

They reached the field hospital in less than half an hour. The driver brought the ambulance to a stop outside a large tent. Lines of wounded men surrounded it, their gauze wrapped wounds stained with blood. Aleksei and the driver lifted Lilia out of the ambulance and carried her toward the front entrance. Amidst the chaos of wounded soldiers, Aleksei got the attention of a doctor.

"I've got a fighter pilot here. She needs attention." Aleksei implored. "She's got some metal in her leg."

The doctor looked curiously at Lilia on the stretcher, pausing for a moment to process the words.

"This way." The doctor finally replied. He then led them into the tent, past a row of tables to one in a corner. "Set her down here. We'll see what we can do." He instructed. "Nurse!" The doctor called out. A Nurse quickly ran over to him. "Prepare this area for surgery. We need to pull some metal out of this pilot's leg."

The nurse also paused for a moment at the realization that the patient was both a woman and a pilot. She then drew a curtain across the corner of the tent.

"Clear the room and sterilize the instruments." The doctor continued.

"Yes, Doctor." The nurse replied, then turned to Aleksei and the driver. "Please wait over here." She said, directing them to an area just outside the tent.

"Please be careful. She's important, this one," said Aleksei.

"We'll do our best. You can be sure." The nurse assured him.

Half an hour later the doctor appeared outside the tent where Aleksei had been sitting, waiting for news. He stood to greet the doctor.

"We pulled the metal from her leg, stopped the bleeding and sterilized the wound. The injury was quite serious." The doctor explained.

"Will she recover?" Aleksei asked.

"There is only so much we can do here. She'll need to see a specialist for further surgery." The doctor replied. "My staff radioed in the request to central command. It was approved almost immediately. She'll be seeing the best specialist in Moscow. She really must be important."

"Very much so." Aleksei answered.

The doctor led Aleksei back inside the tent. "You can see her now."

Aleksei entered the tent to find Lilia unconscious on a cot, with fresh bandages on her leg.

"The anesthetic should be wearing off. She'll be awake soon. We'll have her on the next train." Said the doctor as he stepped away.

"Thank you, doctor."

Aleksei knelt by Lilia, waiting for her to wake up. A few minutes later, she began to stir and then opened her eyes to see Aleksei by her side.

"What's happened? Where are we?" Said Lilia, regaining consciousness.

"You're in a field hospital. They pulled a bullet out of your leg." He replied.

Lilia looked down at her bandaged leg, suddenly reminded again by a sting of pain.

"They're sending you to Moscow for surgery." Aleksei explained.

The doctor returned, seeing Lilia awake. "Lieutenant Litvyak, you're awake?" He asked.

"Yes." She answered.

"I've instructed my staff to put you on the next train to Moscow. I've requested you see a specialist. We've done all we can here." The Doctor explained.

"Is it necessary?" Lilia asked.

"It's what is best to be sure your leg will heal properly." Replied the doctor.

"How long will that take?"

"Perhaps a month, maybe two. My staff will take care of everything and get you to the train station to see you off. Best of luck, Lieutenant." The doctor replied before getting back to his work in the busy hospital.

"You'll be away from the front for a little while," said Aleksei.

"Hold the line for me, Kaluga?" Lilia answered.

Aleksei put Lilia's right hand in both of his own. "It seems for now, Lilia, we say goodbye."

"Goodbye, Lyosha."

Chapter 9

The steam locomotive chugged north, returning Lilia to her hometown of Moscow. It was a great reversal in the direction of her life. For the first time in nearly two years she was being taken away from the fight instead of rushing headlong into it. What might Moscow be like after so much time away? Lilia was taken directly to the hospital from the central train station. The hospital itself was filled to capacity. Every bit of space that could fit a bed did. Every room and hallway was filled with soldiers in various states of recovery. Yet it was not at all like the front. Though chaotic, there was some order and cleanliness to it. A nurse appeared before Lilia as though she had been expected.

"Lieutenant Litvyak?" the nurse asked softly.

"Yes," Lilia replied, holding herself up with a crutch.

"This way please," the nurse replied, leading her down the hall.

A day later, Lilia lay in a hospital bed. Across the room was a small window that offered a glimpse of scattered clouds and a piece of the city's skyline. Patches of snow were still scattered around Moscow, in parks and on sidewalks. The sun would come out for a day and melt some of it away. The next day clouds would appear and bring a light dust of snow flurries. By shooting down the Junckers 88, she had earned her fourth star. The Messerschmitt 109 would be her fifth. Lilia Litvyak had returned to her hometown as the world's first female ace.

The nurse had helped prepare Lilia for further the surgery to her leg. She was washed and dressed in a hospital gown. The bandages from the field hospital were removed and her wound was cleaned and lightly dressed. The surgeon had assessed the damage to her leg and devised a plan to put her back together as Lilia slept through the night. The nurse returned again mid-morning with a wheelchair. "The doctor is ready for you now," she said.

Lilia's wound had been numbed, yet she grit her teeth at the prickling sensation of the surgeon at work. She stared at the ceiling, letting her mind escape to somewhere else. With the nurse by his side, the surgeon worked diligently in repairing Lilia's leg, and carefully made stitches over his work. When he finished, he instructed the nurse to wrap the wound in fresh gauze.

"We must keep this very still for at least a few days." The doctor said quietly to the nurse. The nurse then put a brace on Lilia's leg to keep it straight. The doctor turned to Lilia. "How do you feel?" He asked.

Lilia returned her consciousness to the hospital and the moment, looking down at the leg brace and fresh gauze. "It's a bit numb," she replied.

"You may feel a little pain when the anesthetic wears off. The nurse will give you something for it." The doctor continued.

The nurse and doctor then lifted her from the operating table to the wheel chair.

"How long will it take to heal?" Lilia asked.

"That's hard to say. We'll see how it goes." The doctor answered before the nurse wheeled her out of the room.

"How long will I be in this hospital?" Lilia asked the nurse as she helped Lilia back into the hospital bed.

"I don't know," the nurse answered politely.

Lilia lay in bed for a week, with her small window to look out, and time to think about the entire world and her place in it. While the pain subsided, the boredom consumed her. When the nurse made the daily rounds Lilia asked again how long they intended to keep her.

"That's not for me to say. You'll have to ask the doctor," was the reply. Was she a patient or a prisoner? To high command she was neither. She had become an invaluable military asset in the greatest war the world had ever known.

On the seventh day, Lilia caught the doctor's attention. "Doctor, my mother lives here in Moscow. I would like to finish my recovery at home." She pleaded. The doctor paused at her request. Lilia sensed his hesitation, as though he had been given direct orders in conflict with it. "There must be another soldier who needs this bed?" Lilia implored. The doctor shook his head, straining for an answer. "Please, I promised my mother she would see me again." Lilia followed.

The doctor finally nodded, allowing her request. "You must come in once a week, the next four weeks, so we can check on your progress." Said the doctor.

"Of course." Lilia replied.

Lilia put on her uniform-still cut and blood-stained, and was given a set of crutches. A short ride by streetcar brought her to the family apartment on Novoslobodskaya. Though they had exchanged many letters, many months had passed since Lilia had seen her mother and brother. She navigated her way up the front steps to the door and knocked. Lilia's mother Anna opened it to find Lilia standing before her.

"Lilia!" Anna cried out, and kissed her cheeks.

"Hello, Mamushka." Lilia replied. Anna stepped back a moment, noticing the crutches and Lilia's bandaged leg. Yuri had heard his mother cry out and came in from another room. His face lit up at the sight of his older sister.

"Lilia!" Yuri called out.

"Hello, Yuri." Lilia answered.

"Your leg…" Anna said, appraising the torn and blood-stained uniform, then bit her lip so as not to cry.

"I was injured. They sent me to Moscow for surgery." Lilia replied.

Anna pursed her lips.

"I'll recover. I had the surgery already. They've given me four weeks." Lilia continued.

"Come inside," said Anna, then ushered Lilia into the apartment and into a comfortable chair, putting her crutches aside. It was a mixed blessing for Anna. She hated the thought of her daughter being injured, yet relished the thought that she would be home again for nearly a month.

Her dinner that evening was the first home-cooked meal Lilia had eaten in over a year. Yuri sat across from his sister in awe. He had read every article about her in the newspapers and magazines and kept them all in a red binder. If Lilia was considered a hero to the people, the sentiment was held tenfold by her younger brother. After dinner, Yuri brought out his binder full of clippings for Lilia to see, absolute proof of his sister's fame. The first article he showed her was of the German Ace she had shot down and later confronted at Stalingrad, along with the drawing of her standing before him.

"Listen to the things they write about you," said Yuri, before reading aloud with pride from another article. "When she screams up on alert with her Yakovlev fighter into the blue sky, it seems like the fiery god of vengeance himself, posing as a Russian girl, flying out to deliver judgment and brutal punishment to the hated invaders."

Lilia smiled at her brother. "Yurka, you've gotten so much bigger since I saw you last," said Lilia, changing the subject then hugging him.

The next day, Anna Litvyak went to work washing and repairing Lilia's uniform, still torn and caked with dried blood. Anna soaked the uniform in the kitchen sink, finally getting it to release the stains, turning the water dark amber. While Anna expertly repaired Lilia's uniform, Yuri gathered together her medals. He cleaned and polished each one like a piece of precious jewelry, The Order of the Red Star, and The Order of the Red Banner. When the uniform was stitched back together, freshly washed and mended, and medals reattached, Anna and Yuri laid it out for Lilia on the dining room table.

"Let us see you in it," said Anna.

Lilia took the uniform into her room and changed out of the civilian clothes she had worn for a day and put on her uniform. Lilia stood in the living room of the family apartment, a crutch under one arm, in her uniform and cap. Anna smiled proudly.

"Well, how do I look?" Lilia asked.

"Like a hero." Yuri said reverently.

Lilia had seen the newspaper and magazine articles. They were real enough. But what did it really mean? Would she be recognized on the streets of Moscow? She needed to know. After a week of rest in the family apartment, Lilia grew restless. "I should like to go for a walk," she told Anna. "I need to see Moscow again, to see if it's the same as I remember."

As Lilia walked through her old neighborhood, she studied the expressions of the people who walked past her. The shadows of fear from the time of the purges seemed to have slipped away in the face of war. Some people even dared a passing smile or a nod, yet they couldn't know or understand the things she had seen and done at the front line without having seen it for themselves. Lilia focused on the sounds of the city in relative calm, the grinding of truck gears and streetcars, or the chirping of birds returning in spring.

Lilia spent the next two weeks taking walks around Moscow while recovering in the Litvyak family's apartment, and checking in at the hospital. The crutches were replaced with a cane after her second week. As Lilia walked through a park, her limp slightly improving, she passed an old woman who stopped curiously and stared at her. The old woman certainly did recognize her. She recalled in her mind a night years before. Lilia stared back, waiting for her to speak, but there were no words. The old woman suddenly realized where she had seen Lilia before. She had been present the night Lilia's father was taken away. She had watched and said nothing, another face in a crowd. She had allowed herself to believe at the time, the comforting thought that the charges must be true. Vladimir Litvyak must in fact have been guilty. But there was Lilia, the daughter of an alleged enemy of the people, standing in front of her in a uniform adorned with medals. It didn't add up. At the bottom of her thoughts the old woman felt a sense of shame in her failing to understand it. She half-smiled and bowed awkwardly at Lilia, then turned down her eyes and scurried away.

With each passing day Lilia found the mood of the city to be dark. Although the nearest German was 300 kilometers away, everyone's mind was on the war. There were rations for food and a curfew in place. Each apartment was allotted only a single electric light bulb. As much power as possible must be given to the munitions plants, aircraft, tank, and truck factories. Everyone worked long, tedious hours, to supply the Red Army with what it needed to continue. Even children had wartime jobs to pick up the slack, washing dishes, or cleaning floors. It was everyone's war. Everyone was fighting it, and everyone was a prisoner to it. The fight was for civilization itself, and for any civilization to survive, so must its works of art. There was no room for any form of frivolous fun. The only real entertainment to be found in Moscow in the spring of 1943 was the full ballet performance of Tchaikovsky's Swan Lake at the Bolshoi Theater that ran every other evening. Lilia, wanting to see the best side of Moscow, bought three tickets.

Anna and Yuri put on their best clothes, while Lilia pressed and straightened her uniform for the occasion. The three took a streetcar in the afternoon. Yuri beamed with pride in accompanying his sister, the war hero, to the opulent Bolshoi Theater. Anna, Lilia and Yuri held hands as they ascended the front steps, adorned with enormous white columns. They found their seats amidst the towering red and gold interior, boxes of seats rising up to the ceiling of the massive theater. Built in 1825, in the time of the Tsars, it represented a level of grandiose excess no building created in the Soviet era would rival.

Lilia sat in rapt attention as dozens of ballerinas floated across the stage to the orchestral score. The performances built slowly to the tragic finale, ever-quickening violins, and the eventual deaths of Seigfried and the Swan Princess, Odette. The war seemed far away.

Anna, Lilia, and Yuri rode the streetcar home in silence, none wanting to break the spell. Anna held Lilia's hand with the hint of a smile on her face. Yuri sat quietly next to her as the streetcar traveled along, it's bell ringing from time to time. As the buildings passed, Lilia's thoughts returned to the front, and it was then she made up her mind to return to her regiment the following morning.

After a late supper, Anna washed dishes while Lilia returned to her room to visit her old things by candle light, dresses, photos from her childhood, a piece of jewelry. Yuri entered carrying his red binder and stood silent in front of her. "I'm leaving in the morning," said Lilia in a whisper. "I haven't told her yet."

"She'll be upset. It's a week early." Yuri replied. Lilia nodded. "Tell her in the morning. Let her have one more night's sleep," Yuri continued. Lilia nodded again. "You've made the papers again," said Yuri, opening his red binder. Inside was a fresh newspaper clipping. The article detailed her downing of the Junckers 88, and her face off with the Messerschmitt 109s. "You've got five, Lilia. You're an ace now. They can never take that away." Yuri announced.

"Take care of our mother, Yurka," said Lilia, as she put her arms around him.

Lilia was up before dawn as she had been every day at the front. She brewed a pot of tea while Anna slept and waited for the sun to rise. Half an hour after daylight, Anna emerged in a robe to find Lilia sitting at the table in her uniform.

"How long have you been up?" Asked Anna.

"I've been waiting for you to wake up so I could say goodbye." Lilia replied.

"You're leaving?"

"I'm going back to my regiment." Lilia answered.

"It's only been three weeks. You can stay another week," Anna replied.

Lilia didn't want to argue and Anna knew she couldn't win. In their time apart Lilia's will had turned to iron. Anna sensed another change in her daughter had already taken place. She asked only one further question.

"What is his name?"

Chapter 10

Lilia Litvyak returned to the 73rd Guards regiment on the 19th of April, 1943.

She had traveled the distance from Moscow to Rostov-on-Don by train then found a ride in the back of a supply truck. She stepped down from the truck, steadying herself with her cane, and walked toward the command bunker with a limp. Katya stood by her airplane in the lineup and spotted Lilia as she approached.

"Lilka!" Katya yelled out, then shouted down the lineup. "Tell the Colonel that Lieutenant Litvyak has returned."

Lilia stopped to greet her. "Yes, I'm back." Lilia answered.

"Good to have you back, little sister." Katya replied.

The news travelled quickly down the lineup and into the command bunker. Aleksei stepped out, followed by Colonel Baranov, and walked over to greet her. Aleksei did his best to contain his feelings, but the smile on his face betrayed him.

"Lieutenant Litvyak, welcome back," said Colonel Baranov.

"Thank you, Colonel." Replied Lilia.

"How are you feeling?" asked Baranov.

"I'm not quite ready to fly yet. I need a few more days to heal." Lilia replied.

"As much time as you need." The Colonel answered then stepped away.

"This war hasn't been the same without you," said Aleksei before they kissed each other on both cheeks.

Sasha Martinov walked over, flight helmet in hand. "Hey, look who's back!"

"Sasha and I have a mission to fly," said Aleksei. Sasha immediately saw the worry on Lilia's face, though she tried to conceal it.

"Don't worry, Lilia. I've got his wing covered," said Sasha, and Lilia's look of worry dissipated for the moment. "Try to stay off the leg. You'll be back in the air in no time," he continued.

Lilia turned to Aleksei, "Keep the Fritzes busy, Kaluga."

"I'll be back for supper. You can tell me about Moscow," he replied.

Lilia couldn't help but to watch the skies, knowing how long their supply of fuel would last from take off. Three weeks apart had given her a new perspective. Back at the airbase everything suddenly felt real and immediate again. As the minutes counted by Lilia checked her watch for time. Fifteen minutes after take off Colonel Baranov joined Lilia by the aircraft lineup, also looking at his watch, awaiting the return of his pilots.

Several minutes later the pair of Yaks returned to base and touched down. Sasha and Aleksei pulled their airplanes into the lineup and stepped down from the wings. Sasha walked over to Lilia, grinning. He waited as Aleksei joined them.

"Did the Fritzes give you any trouble?" Lilia asked.

Sasha stepped forward. "Our boy, Aleksei, did some fantastic flying up there. Two more stars on his plane!"

Colonel Baranov, standing nearby, was particularly pleased to hear of Aleksei's new victories. "Very good," the Colonel said aloud. "Sasha, you'll type the report."

"Of course," Sasha replied with a grin. "Typing duty, again."

In the evening, after the last sorties had returned and the pilots had gathered in the canteen for dinner. Colonel Baranov stood up to make an announcement, banging a spoon on a tin cup to get their attention. "Here, here!" Baranov said aloud, quickly bringing the bunker to silence. Lilia and Aleksei sat together in a corner, breaking off their conversation at the sound of Baranov's voice. "Attention, everyone," said the Colonel after catching the eyes of every pilot present. "Captain Solomatin, please step forward," the Colonel continued.

"What is this now?" Aleksei said to Lilia as he stood. Baranov grinned, enjoying the spectacle. "What now, Kolya?" said Aleksei as he stepped forward.

Baranov then held up a small ornate red box in one hand, and a certificate in the other. "I made a request to High Command, with the details of your victories. That request has been granted." Baranov replied then began to read the certificate aloud.

"In acknowledgement of your fearless courage in the face of danger, for acts of heroism in service of the Soviet state, you are hereby, officially declared now and forever a Hero of the Soviet Union."

A howl roared through the bunker as the other pilots clapped and cheered. Colonel Baranov then opened the small red box to reveal a star made of gold attached to a red ribbon. The Colonel took out the medal and affixed it to the upper left chest of Aleksei's uniform. "Congratulations," said Baranov warmly.

"Thank you, Kolya."

After the commotion died down and the other pilots had offered Aleksei their personal congratulations, adjourning for the night, Baranov stopped Lilia as she passed.

"Lieutenant Litvyak, a word please," said the Colonel.

"Yes?"

"I want you to know that I sent a request to Command that you receive the award as well. It was declined, for now." Baranov explained. Lilia nodded. "We'll put some more stars on your plane and submit again. Let me know when you're ready to fly and I'll put you back on the roster," he continued.

"Thank you, Colonel."

Later that evening, laying on a cot in Aleksei's bunker, Lilia stared at the gold star on his uniform. "So you're a hero now?" She said.

Aleksei chuckled, "…And forever," he replied then unfastened the gold star.

"Can I hold it?" asked Lilia.

"Of course, you're holding my heart, Lilia. What is this in comparison, a piece of metal?" Aleksei watched her as she held the gold star, staring at it in reverence. It was, after all, the nation's highest honor.

"Congratulations. You earned it."

"You were promised one as well, and you'll have it. Kolya is a good man. He always keeps his word." Aleksei answered.

In the evening of the following day, Lilia found the Colonel in the canteen. "I'm ready for duty again, Colonel," said Lilia.

"Are you sure that leg has healed up?" He asked.

"Yes, Colonel," she replied.

Colonel Baranov nodded. "I'll put you back on the roster. Briefing in the command bunker in half an hour on tomorrow's mission." He followed.

During Lilia's time away from the front line the objectives of the war had changed. The German war machine required massive amounts of fuel to continue fighting. No amount of tanks and planes and trucks, nor how technologically advanced they may be would make any difference without enough fuel to run them. The objective of the German Army's push to take and hold Stalingrad had been to gain control of the oil fields of the Caucasus to the south. When the objective failed, they had devised a new one.

By early 1943, German scientists had developed a process by which to synthesize gasoline from coal. After their previous plan to keep the German war machine going with gasoline made from the oil of the Caucasus had failed, their new objective was to do so with gasoline made from the coal in the Donetsk Basin, known as the Donbass. The crux of the war now balanced on the fight for the Donbass coal.

Lilia and the other pilots assembled in the command bunker as Colonel Baranov, standing before a large map on the wall, laid out the bomber escort mission for the following day. "They're making every effort possible now to get control of the coal fields of the Donbass. We will stop them, as we did at Stalingrad," declared the Colonel. "Our intelligence sources have identified the supply route and believe a column will be on the move before dawn." The Colonel continued, pointing out the location on the map. "We take off at first light, and rendezvous with the PE-2s. Our objective is for the PE-2s to catch the column by surprise and hit it in a single bombing run. I'll fly the lead on this mission. Mikhail will fly on my wing. Sasha, you'll fly with Budanova, and Aleksei, you'll have Lieutenant Litvyak back on your wing."

Aleksei found Lilia outside the bunker after the briefing, a look of worry on his face. "Back in the fight already?" He asked of her.

"My leg is healed. I'm ready to fly again." Lilia replied. Aleksei nodded, knowing an argument was pointless. "You'll have my wing tomorrow, and I'll have yours," Lilia followed.

Ina had Lilia's Yak-1 fueled and ready before dawn the next morning. In the still darkness, Lilia approached the airplane, her limp evident. "How's the leg?" Asked Ina.

"Strong enough," Lilia replied as she handed Ina her cane.

Lilia and Aleksei climbed into their airplanes and strapped into the cockpits. Ground crews unblocked the wheels and pushed the fighter planes into position at the end of the runway. The formation of six sat in their cockpits waiting for the sun to come up, and the order from the Colonel to start their engines.

As the sky began to light up, Baranov checked his watch. It was 5:22 AM.

"Engines up!" The Colonel commanded over the radio. The six Yak engines cranked over and their propellers spun into a blur. The Yaks took off in pairs and climbed just high enough to see the edge of the sun cresting the eastern horizon. They pulled into formation and turned north. "Hold formation, and follow my lead." Baranov called over the radio. "We'll meet the bombers before we cross the line."

Across the faint orange morning horizon, the formation of fifteen Petylyakov-2 twin-engine attack bombers came into view. Colonel Baranov pulled the six Yaks alongside the lead bomber, waggled his wings and hailed their commander over the radio.

"Contact, your escort has arrived." Baranov spoke through the pre-arranged channel.

"Good morning, Colonel." Replied their commander.

"The Seventy-Third Guard has you covered, Captain. Proceed to target." Answered Colonel Baranov.

The Yaks pulled up and above the formation and matched their speed. With the dawn still breaking, the PE-2 bombers and their Yak-1 fighter planes flying high cover turned west over the Donbass and across the front line. "Take your positions." Baranov ordered over the radio.

The six Yaks split into pairs and moved to cover the lead and sides above the bomber formation. They flew past rows of soldiers in trenches, tanks and trucks, first of the Red Army, and then of the German. They flew on several minutes deeper across the line in search of their target. Flying over a dirt road that moved through hills, past thickets of trees and farmland, the Bomber Captain called out over the radio. "Target in sight. Open bomb bay doors." He ordered.

The German supply column came into view one thousand meters below, Panzer tanks, trucks, half-tracks, and artillery pieces meant to smash through the line and take the coal fields for their own. They looked like small toys at such distance, and the soldiers on foot around them like scattering ants. The column stretched over half a kilometer. Panic erupted along the column as the German soldiers spotted the incoming bombers.

"Bombers!" a German soldier called out, pointing to the sky.

The bombers tightened their formation further on the approach, each bombardier lining up their targeting scope. The orders were given and one by one the bombers dropped their payloads in a curtain of bombs. The morning stillness was shattered as the bombs hit their targets in a sweeping mass of explosions the entire length of the supply column. The lead bomber flew over the end of the column then banked hard left. The rest of the formation followed.

While the bombers made their turn, a formation of Messerschmitt 109s appeared, diving toward them.

"Fighters, nine o'clock high!" Aleksei shouted over the radio. Aleksei kicked the pedals and pulled the stick over hard left to make the intercept. Lilia followed tight on his wing position. Aleksei fired a gun burst, shredding the tail section of a diving Messerschmitt. The other three broke off their attack on the bombers and turned to meet the Yaks. Before they could reach a head to head face off, Lilia put one in her sights and let out a burst of gunfire. Flames exploded from the Messerschmitt's engine, trailing black smoke as it dropped out of the fight.

Another formation of four Messerschmitt 109s dove in from a high position on Sasha and Katya, bullets streaking down toward them. "Breaking right, Blackbird! Stay on my wing." Sasha called out over the radio, breaking hard right and away from the incoming fire. Katya held position as they rolled over to catch the Messers near the bottom of the diving attack. The Messers banked hard left to counter, splitting in opposite directions. The two Yaks and the four Messers all banked in hard turns to re-engage, coming head to head.

"Go straight at them! Hold steady!" Katya shouted, firing a steady stream of bullets. The Messers broke formation, fanning out in pairs. Katya's bullets ripped through the underbelly of an enemy fighter, hitting the fuel tank, exploding it into a fireball.

While the bombers had made their escape, the Yaks stayed to tangle with the fighters over the smoldering wreckage of what had been the German supply column. The soldiers that survived the bombing run pulled themselves from the sides of the road to watch the battle in the sky above. It was a chaotic scene of multiple pairs of fighters engaged in separate dogfights in the same airspace. One soldier pulled himself up to find a 20mm anti-aircraft gun mounted on the back of a truck that had somehow survived the bombing run. He manned the gun, aiming at the sky, while trying to make sense of the chaotic air battle above.

While Lilia and Aleksei managed to chase off some remaining enemy fighters, Baranov and Mikhail were locked in a descending spiral. Aleksei spotted the gunner below after a streak of orange shot through the Colonel's tail section.

"Kolya, climb! They've got an anti-aircraft gun down there." Aleksei shouted over the radio.

Mikhail pulled back on the stick as hard as a he could. "We're closing on them!" Mikhail shouted.

"Stay on my wing," answered the Colonel. The Colonel was determined to use the Yak fighter's lighter weight and tighter turn radius to gain the advantage, but their loss of altitude had put them in range of the gunner below. More orange streaks shot through the Colonel's engine. It caught fire and was quickly pouring out black smoke.

Lilia and Aleksei fired at the Messers getting around on the Colonel. The enemy fighters flipped over in tandem and dove, ducking out of the fight.

"You're clear. Get out of there!" Aleksei declared.

Mikhail kicked the pedals and turned to climb, while Colonel Baranov's fate was sealed. His airplane sputtered and fell, flames wrapping around its nose and pouring smoke. It crashed to the ground below in a burst of orange flames.

"Kolya!" Aleksei cried out.

The bombers had already made their escape back across the line, and the remaining Messers had quit the fight. With Baranov lost, Aleksei gave the order.

"Break it off. Back to base." The Yaks re-grouped in formation and turned east.

News of the loss of Colonel Baranov travelled quickly, manifesting as a darkened mood and a deep loss of confidence across the airbase. Aleksei and Sasha paced in the command bunker, pondering the next move. "Should I write the report?" Sasha asked.

"I'll write it. We'll have to inform command." Aleksei replied.

"You're the ranking officer now." Sasha replied.

Aleksei sat down at the Colonel's desk and found a pen and ink and a piece of paper. He began to write by hand, crossing out words and rewriting them. Sasha sat down across from him.

"I'll work the typewriter when you're ready." Said Sasha, cueing a sheet of paper into the machine.

Aleksei held up his sheet of paper and began to read as Sasha typed. "We regret to inform the High Command of the loss of Colonel Nikolai Baranov, commander of the Seventy-Third Guards fighter regiment during bomber escort duties over the Donbass. We await your further instructions, and humbly request Colonel Baranov be awarded the highest honors for bravery in battle, Captain Aleksei Solomatin."

That evening, Lilia and Aleksei lay together in his bunker. He had lost many friends in the war, but somehow this was different. Lilia was surprised to see him so deeply affected. "It's a heavy loss," Lilia said painfully. "We won't have the Colonel watching over us."

"It comes down to us now." Aleksei replied. "If not us, then who? Kolya knew why we're here. He knew what it meant.

The life of a fighter pilot..." Aleksei paused, considering his words. "He knew our fate."

"Must it be our fate?" Asked Lilia.

"Nobody can know the future." Aleksei replied. "But we can be realists."

"I want to believe in the future, that it's possible." Lilia replied. "I had time to imagine it while I was in Moscow, a time we could be husband and wife in a world at peace, a house in the country, or a cottage by the sea." Lilia continued. "I want to believe it."

"So believe in the future, and live for the moment." Aleksei answered then put his forehead against hers. "Live for this moment, and every moment we're given. Now is forever."

Chapter 11

Ina had noticed a change in Mikhail's demeanor since the loss of Colonel Baranov, less jovial, more reticent to make a joke. When they snuck away to his bunker late the following evening, she couldn't restrain herself from asking.

"It was bad luck," he answered with a hint of guilt in his voice. "Why the Colonel and not me?"

"But it wasn't you. You're still here." Ina replied.

The incident may have shaken his nerves, but it hadn't changed his resolve. It was all the more reason to cherish what is here today and not to live in fear of what may be gone tomorrow. Mikhail reached into his shirt pocket, pulled out a small photograph and handed it to Ina. It was the image of a woman in her late thirties next to two teenage girls, standing in front of a small house with a thatched roof. They were all smiling on a summer day. "My mother, and my sisters," he explained.

Ina studied the photograph carefully in the dim light of the bunker.

"It's a small village, but life is good there. It's peaceful. We pick wild cherries in the summer and make vernicki. It's a farm community. We trade with each other in fruit, and jams, and eggs. There's a festival for every season. They sing and play the balalaika while the old men drink vodka and tell their old stories. "He pointed to the photo in Ina's hand. "You'll like them. My mother is kind, and my sisters will make you laugh."

Ina clutched the photograph to her chest.

"Hold on to it for the both of us." He continued.

The next day Sasha entered the command bunker to find Aleksei pacing, still awaiting orders. "Any word from Command?" asked Sasha.

"Nothing. We're effectively on stand down until the new Colonel arrives." Aleksei replied.

"And another day goes by with no missions." Sasha answered.

"There must be gaps in the line. They could send us up as free hunters at least," said Aleksei in frustration.

"Perhaps the line is moving too fast for that. They're waiting to give us more escort missions." Sasha replied.

"Then we'll use this time to get everything fixed, put the whole regiment in top condition, every uniform and piece of equipment. Make sure everything is battle ready. We're still a Guards regiment. Let's be sure we look like one when the new Colonel gets here." Aleksei declared. "Give the orders. Get them moving full speed. He could be here any moment and give us a mission. Let's be ready."

"Of course." Sasha replied.

Aleksei turned to the Radio Operator in a cubby. "Any communications come through, I want to know about it right away."

"Yes, captain." He replied.

Sasha set the flight line into a frenzy, giving the orders to get every plane fully armed and fueled, and fully repaired. Armorers, mechanics and ground crews set to work patching bullet holes, adjusting cables, and refueling the planes.

At noon, Aleksei and Lilia sat in the canteen for lunch, taking a break from the bustle of the flight line. "We did real damage to the fascists destroying that column, though we lost the Colonel for it," said Aleksei. "They still have their aces up there, but we're seeing a lot of their pilots without much experience."

"What do you think it means?" asked Lilia.

"It means they're running out of recruits. It means we're winning the war now. It's only a matter of time. We'll see it through to the end, all the way to Berlin."

"Why do you sound like such an optimist all of a sudden?" Lilia asked.

"Maybe you were right. Some hope for the future isn't a bad thing. We're fighting for it. I suppose I'd like to believe I might get to enjoy it when it arrives." Aleksei answered.

"What does it look like?" She asked.

"We'll go to Moscow as heroes, and then a cottage by the sea."

"How do we get there, Lyosha?" She asked.

"We do our best flying yet. We stick together, and make all the right moves." He replied.

Throughout the afternoon, a Radio Operator remained on shift inside the command bunker, monitoring any chatter he could discern from the frontline. He would hear in staccato, the frantic voices of air battles and attack bombers engaged in ground support. Aleksei checked in hourly to ask if any orders from command had been issued. "Nothing, Captain," was the reply. Aleksei then returned to supervising the lineup, checking on readiness of aircraft and pilots.

Fayina had been given the clearance to do engine work on Lilia's airplane. "I'm going to rebuild the carburetors and clean the fuel system today, Lilia," she said, pushing a stepladder under the nose of the aircraft. She began by unscrewing and removing the engine cowlings. She laid them neatly beside her tool cart, then climbed back on the ladder to assess the massive Klimov engine, finding the fuel lines to disconnect them from the carburetors.

As Fayina worked, Lilia pulled out a pen and paper to write a letter as she sat on the wing. "A letter home?" Fayina asked.

"Do you think the papers will mention that we lost the Colonel?" Lilia replied.

"I doubt it. They only print the good news." Fayina answered.

"My brother should like to know about it. He's gathering every piece of news he can find in a scrapbook," said Lilia, contemplating her thoughts before setting pen to paper.

While Fayina continued disconnecting the carburetor linkage, Mikhail appeared. "Looks like you're giving Lilia's aircraft the full treatment."

"I'm going to get this bird flying perfectly." Fayina answered. Lilia watched them together, noticing how they concealed their affection for one another.

"I'll let you work then." Mikhail answered with a smile then continued toward his airplane.

At mid-afternoon, while Aleksei was inspecting the lineup, a new set of chatter was heard over the radio. The radio operator called a technician over. "Come listen to this."

"What is it?"

"I don't know yet." He answered. " One of our pilots somewhere across the line called out a formation of bombers and fighters. No location or direction given. He couldn't engage. He hadn't the fuel or ammunition for it."

"When was this?" the technician asked.

"Just now, a minute ago." The radio operator answered, looking at his watch. "Go and get Captain Solomatin."

"Right away," he replied, and rushed out of the bunker.

The technician ran to the lineup, to find Aleksei by the Chief Armorer, ordering inventories of ammunition stocks. "Captain Solomatin, come quickly. We may have something on the comms." He said, nearly out of breath.

"Is it orders from Command?" Aleksei asked.

"No. Bombers and fighters headed for the line."

In the command bunker, the radio operator continued to listen. "Location, please. Give me your location." He broadcast. The chatter came back with the name of a village. He quickly found it on a map, placing his finger on it. "Heading?" What's the heading?" He pressed.

Aleksei entered the bunker and rushed to the Radio Operator. "What have you got?" Aleksei asked.

"A formation of bombers and fighters, heading south." He answered, then pointed to a spot on the map and checked his watch. "First spotted in this area four minutes ago, Captain." He pointed to two more points on the map. "We have spotters, here, and here."

"Coordinates? Give me coordinates," said Aleksei.

"They crossed the line unopposed, here." He pointed to another spot on the map, continuing to listen through the headset.

More chatter was heard. "Bombers... Fighters..."

"Again, just now." He relayed then called out. "Location?" The radio operator implored, then quickly pointed to another spot on the map, extrapolating their direction. "Captain, they're heading straight for us."

"Direction?" Aleksei ordered.

The radio operator calculated. "Northwest, three-one-seven."

Aleksei ran out of the command bunker toward the lineup. "Engines up! We've got incoming!" Aleksei shouted. The orders were quickly repeated with a series of shouts down the line.

Katya, Mikhail, and Sasha strapped on their flight helmets and jumped in their cockpits.

As Aleksei passed Lilia's aircraft, she called out, standing on its wing. "What's happening?" asked Lilia.

"Incoming, bombers and fighters." Aleksei replied, then paused a second at the sight of Lilia's aircraft in pieces, engine cowlings on the ground. Aleksei ran to his airplane and jumped in the cockpit.

"Fayina, put it all back together, quickly!" Lilia ordered. Fayina scrambled to finish the job, knowing it was an impossible order. It had taken her more than hour to pull the Yak apart to begin to the work.

The other Yak's engines fired up. Their wheels unblocked, one by one, they taxied out of the lineup. Lilia caught a last glance of Aleksei in his cockpit as he taxied to the runway. "Hurry, Fayina!" Lilia pleaded, strapping on her flight helmet.

Fayina in a mad rush, called out to another mechanic for help. "We have to get Lilia up in the air." She shouted.

The mechanic rushed to help, pulling his stepladder under the nose of the Lilia's fighter plane. He climbed up next to Fayina to assess the work to be done. The fuel lines and throttle linkage were still disconnected.

Lilia strapped on her parachute harness and climbed into the cockpit. "How much time, Fayina?" Lilia asked.

"A few minutes, Lilia." Fayina answered, working on the throttle linkage, while the other mechanic worked quickly to reconnect the fuel lines.

Lilia strapped herself into the cockpit then turned on the radio. She put on the headset to listen, hearing what sounded like Katya's voice. "Matching speed, Captain. On your wing."

Aleksei responded. "Hold formation, heading three one seven, until we find the target."

"I don't see anything. They should be here." Sasha Martinov added.

"Should we circle, Captain?" Katya asked.

"No, hold the course." Aleksei replied.

Fayina and the other mechanic worked feverishly as Lilia sat in the cockpit listening to the headset.

"There! Two o'clock, low!" Katya yelled out.

"Correcting course. Stay on my wing!" Aleksei could be heard.

"Don't lose them." Sasha replied. "Increasing speed."

"Hit their five o'clock, and watch the top turrets." Aleksei ordered.

Lilia took off the headset and put her head out of her cockpit. "How much longer, Fayina?" she asked.

"A few more minutes." Fayina replied.

Lilia put the headset back on to hear Katya call out in a stern voice. "I'm going in!"

The radio began to cut out and cut back in again, with the crackle of machine gun fire, the rumble of engines amidst voices and static.

"Making another pass!" a voice called out.

"Switching to cannon." Katya called, followed by loud thumps.

Aleksei's voice called out, "Fighters! Up high!"

"I see them." Sasha was heard.

"Coming around." Called another voice.

Lilia listened closely through the headset, powerless to do anything. She looked out of the cockpit to see engine cowlings still on the ground.

Katya's stern voice crackled across the static. "Watch those fighters!"

"On your six!" said another.

"Break right!" another followed.

Lilia pulled her head out of the cockpit again. "How much longer?" she asked.

"Almost ready." Fayina replied, then stepped down from the ladder to pick up one of the engine cowlings.

Lilia returned her attention to the radio. The voices were more frantic still. "Steady! Close the gap!" she heard Aleksei say, followed the rattling sound of machine gun fire.

"He's down!"

"Break away!"

"Let them run!"

"I'm hit!"

"Break it off."

"Break away! Break away!"

The radio suddenly dropped out and all Lilia could hear was static. She tried to tune it back in, yet found no trace of their voices. She took off the headset and looked out to see Fayina and the other mechanic carrying an engine cowling. She sat back in the cockpit and put the headset back on, tuning the radio again trying to hear their voices, only to find static. She set the radio back to the channel then called out. "This is Seagull ninety, respond." She waited then repeated. "This is Seagull ninety, please respond."

Another moment of silence passed. Lilia dropped her head, fearing the worst, then repeated again. "This is Seagull ninety, please respond."

Silence.

Fayina and the other mechanic had almost finished affixing the cowlings when the radio suddenly came to life again. "It's over. We're on our way back." Lilia heard in what sounded like Aleksei's voice.

Lilia sat back in relief, then unstrapped her seat belt and climbed out of the cockpit onto the wing. She stepped down from the wing to watch the sky at the end of the runway.

"What's happening?" Asked Fayina.

"They're coming back." Lilia replied.

Fayina and the other mechanic finished tightening down the last bolts on the engine cowling.

Fayina returned the wrenches to her tool cart and wiped the grease from her hands with a rag.

A few minutes passed before they heard the familiar rumble of Klimov engines in the distance, growing louder as the Yaks returned to base. They glided in and landed, then taxied into the lineup. Ground crews blocked the wheels, and the propellers came to a stop. Quiet returned to the airfield as Aleksei stepped down from the wing of his airplane. Lilia watched as Katya and Sasha joined him at the edge of the runway. They huddled together for a moment. Aleksei calmly took out his pistol and raised it in the air. He pulled the trigger and let out the crack of a single shot. The mechanics and ground crew all paused what they were doing to notice. Aleksei, Sasha, and Katya turned and walked toward the command bunker, Aleksei stopping next to Lilia's airplane.

"What's happened?" Lilia asked.

"We lost Mikhail, somewhere across the line." Aleksei replied then continued toward the command bunker.

Lilia turned around to see Fayina on her knees, her face covered in tears. Lilia ran and put her arms around her, holding her as she wept. Mikhail was gone, another pilot to be forgotten, lost behind the line. Fayina finally looked up toward a patch of sky beyond the end of the runway, tears rolling down her cheeks. "Ina..." said Lilia, softly. "Ina..."

Chapter 12

Reports of the Luftwaffe raid had reached High Command by the evening. On Aleksei's orders, the radio operators had transmitted his request that the 73rd Guards be given permission to fly free hunting missions over the front line. The following morning, his request was granted. Aleksei emerged from the command bunker to find Lilia by her aircraft in the line up. "We're back to free hunting," he announced. Lilia nodded. "Better we should choose our targets, than our targets choose us." Aleksei continued.

"Ready for duty, Captain." Lilia replied.

"Get the airplane armed, and fueled, and ready. We'll take the first flight. We're up in twenty minutes. I'll tell the others." Aleksei said, then walked down the line giving the orders, setting the entire regiment in motion, arming and fueling aircraft.

Half an hour later Lilia and Aleksei were approaching the front line, flying as a pair. Aleksei called out to the ground spotters by radio. "This is the free hunting Seventy-third. If you have a target in sight, call it out."

A thin voice responded amidst the chatter. "Seventy-third, come in."

"Seventy-third here." Aleksei replied.

"Enemy aircraft spotted, south of Donetsk, heading south, one, five, seven, altitude five thousand meters." The voice followed.

"We're on it." Aleksei answered. "Climbing to five thousand meters."

Aleksei pulled left and climbed, Lilia staying tight on his wing as they flew in formation through light clouds.

"They should be here," said Aleksei.

"I see something, one o'clock." Lilia called out, spotting two black spots in the sky ahead of them.

"I see them. Correcting course." Aleksei replied, making a soft right turn.

The dark specks grew larger as they came closer.

"Can you identify it?" Aleksei asked.

"Not yet." Lilia replied, looking again to see the distinctive outlines of two Messerschmitt 109s heading straight toward them holding their course. "One-o-nines!" Lilia called out.

"Hold my wing." Aleksei replied, pulling into a head to head engagement. "Switching to cannon." Aleksei announced.

The silhouettes of the two marauding Messerschmitts' noses lit up in flashes as they fired, spraying their bullets wildly across the sky. The gap closing quickly, it was a contest to be determined by marksmanship and nerve.

"Steady." Aleksei said as he lined up the shot. Five cannon bursts at the fast approaching fighters set the lead Messerschmitt on fire. The airplane rolled over and dove away, trailing smoke.

The second fighter peeled away hard left, putting its blue underbelly in Lilia's gun sights. She pulled the trigger, a hail of bullets ripping into it. Smoke poured from the nose as it dove, then leveled out below them. The canopy swung open as the aircraft caught fire. Amidst the smoke and flames the pilot pulled himself out and lobbed himself into the sky. Lilia and Aleksei both watched the scene play out as the burning fighter plane trailed black smoke away from the falling pilot. The parachute silk popped open below them as they circled around.

"Our ground forces will pick him up. The war is over for him," said Aleksei. "Back to base."

Ina was cleaning and re-organizing her tool cart when she heard the sound of two returning Yaks. She looked up to spot them past the edge of the airfield, coming in for a landing. While Aleksei touched down and pulled into the line up, Lilia pulled up and flew across the airfield upside down. The mechanics and ground crews cheered.

Aleksei climbed out of his cockpit to watch Lilia flying stunts over the airfield. After another barrel roll, Lilia brought it in for a landing and pulled into the line up. Aleksei was waiting as she climbed out of the cockpit to join him. "Paint another star on the plane, Fayina!" Aleksei said, pointing to the fuselage, as he and Lilia headed for the command bunker.

The new Colonel, Ivan Golyshev, arrived two days later. Upon his arrival at the 73rd Guards, he read all of the recent combat reports including that of the death of his predecessor, Nikolai Baranov. After studying the regiment's recent history at the front, he gathered the entire regiment at the edge of the airfield to introduce himself, and build morale. "The hard work you have all contributed to the war has not gone unnoticed. The High Command has praised your work as a Guards regiment. There are Heroes of the Soviet Union amongst you, and future heroes. I am honored to be your new commander. Together, we fight on! Our future is victory! We will save our Motherland!" he concluded loudly to mechanics, armorers, and ground crews, drawings loud cheers from their ranks.

Afterwards, Golyshev met with the pilots of the regiment in the command bunker. He told them details of his own successes and losses elsewhere on the front, and soon enough they were all speaking of tactics and strategy. "It's the ground game now." Golyshev explained. "We'll be escorting Shturmoviks. We fly high cover while they hit the targets one by one." He brought out the maps, pointing to their objective areas. The Germans had failed to take the Donbass, yet they had succeeded in claiming the city of Kharkov to the north. "Our task is to push this line west and drive them back. We start tomorrow. That's all for now," said Golyshev. As they turned to leave, the Colonel continued. "Come by after supper. Tomorrow we fly into battle together. Tonight, we drink."

Lilia and Aleksei ate their dinner together in the canteen as usual. "What do you think about the new commander?" She asked.

"He seems capable. He has experience. They wouldn't have sent him otherwise. He wants to keep us on the offensive, and let the Germans play defense." Aleksei answered.

After dinner, the sun past the horizon, Lilia excused herself. "You can have my vodka rations." She said.

"You don't want to drink with our new Colonel?" Aleksei asked.

"No, I want to sleep." She explained.

"It's early." Aleksei replied.

"You and Sasha go have your vodka with the Colonel. I want to be well rested for whatever tomorrow brings." She answered.

Aleksei kissed her. "Sleep well," he said, then turned toward the command bunker where Sasha was already standing outside.

Katya had also opted for sleep. "Goodnight, Captain." She said as she walked past Aleksei.

Golyshev set chairs at a table, shot glasses for each, and a bottle of vodka in the middle. "Ah, my heroes of the Soviet Union." He said as Aleksei and Sasha entered the bunker. All three men wore the gold star on the upper left of their uniforms. "Our women pilots not joining us?" He asked.

"They're off to bed. They're more professional than us." Aleksei replied.

Golyshev poured a round of shots then held up his own glass to make a toast.

"To our success in battle together in the Seventy-Third Guards." They all downed the shot and returned their glasses to the table. Golyshev poured another round.

"To destroying the fascist invaders and saving our Motherland."

They drank.

Another round. Another toast. On it went into the night.

They were ready on the line just after dawn the next morning. The mission plan evolved as intelligence reports came in of enemy convoy locations and movements. By mid-morning Aleksei, Lilia, Sasha and Golyshev were flying in a formation of four Yaks to meet Ilyushin-2 ground attack bombers and escort them across the line to their targets. They were first heard over heavy radio chatter in many dialects, with radio operators and spotters coordinating. Shortly after, their paths converged as the bombers came into view, in a formation of twelve, thundering across the sky. Golyshev waggled his wings and ordered the Yaks to high cover.

The Ilyushin-2, otherwise known as the Shturmovik, was a twin engine ground attack bomber, with a heavily armored dual cockpit. The pilot could deploy machine guns, rockets, or bombs to a target from the front, while directly behind him sat a rear gunner. The formation of IL-2s and their escort of Yak-1 fighters continued across the front line. The target they were to find was a short supply column, in motion twenty kilometers behind the line.

Disrupting the supply of food and ammunition, and especially new artillery pieces to the frontline troops provided vitally important support for the ground war. The IL-2 squadron had already mapped and plotted every possible supply route. The Yaks held their position of high cover while the Shturmoviks hunted their target. The supply column came into view as they passed a row of hills, opening to a valley pass, and a row of trucks flanked by troops on foot.

The Shturmoviks began their attack on the flight commander's order, swooping into a highly coordinated pattern of diving figure eights. Rockets streaked into the column, exploding trucks and the ammunition they carried. The radio chatter amongst the IL-2 pilots turned frantic as the Yaks flew into a circular pattern above them.

"Tank!" an IL-2 pilot called out over the radio.

"It's a Panzer," replied another.

"Who has bombs?" Asked their flight commander.

"We've got it," yet another pilot answered.

Several hundred meters in front of the column, a Panzer tank crawled across the valley floor, flanked by a dozen troops on foot. A lone Shturmovik broke from the others to make its bombing run. With a direct hit, the tank exploded and caught fire.

"Fighters!" Golyshev called out.

"Rear gunners on alert! We've got fighters incoming." The IL-2 Captain called out.

"Keep them off the formation!" Ordered Golyshev.

The Yaks turned to engage six Messerschmitt 109s diving on the Shturmoviks, firing a barrage of bullets. The Messerschmitts split their formation in two, turning up to face the Yaks. As the Shturmoviks continued their attack on the supply column, the fighters above them flew into a chaotic mass of interwoven dogfights.

"Seagull, Messerschmitt on your six." Aleksei called out as bullets streaked past Lilia's cockpit.

While the Messerschmitt pilot tried to put Lilia in his gun sights, three IL-2 gunners had heard the call out. They swiveled their guns, all three firing upwards at the Messerschmitt, punching holes in its wings. Lilia watched in the mirror as an orange fireball blew out of the Messerschmitt's undercarriage. It dove away quickly, and out of the fight. Bullets streaked across the sky in all directions between the fighters, with barrages from below as twelve Shturmovik rear gunners picked their targets.

The Shturmoviks made their final pass, leaving the column a mass of flaming wreckage. Rockets and bombs nearly expended, their mission was complete. The IL-2 flight commander gave the order. "They're finished. Shturmoviks back to base."

The IL-2s regrouped into formation and pushed full throttle back across the line. Four Messerschmitts remained in the sky above the burning supply column. They suddenly broke off their own attack, diving away to split for the west. "Let them go." Ordered Golyshev. "Seventy-third, back to base."

The Yaks flew back into formation and turned southeast. The Germans had lost two fighter planes and a supply column, while every Shturmovik and Yak had returned to base.

Aleksei stood by the wing of Lilia's airplane to help her down as Golyshev walked down the line up. He nodded to Lilia and Aleksei then stopped to sum up the mission with a single word. "Success." The new colonel then called over to Alexander Martinov. "Come Sasha, help me write this report." He said as they marched toward the command bunker.

Aleksei picked up Lilia to carry her down from the wing and put her on her feet, before noticing three bullet holes in the fuselage.

Fayina pulled her tool cart past the wing to find Aleksei staring at them as though they represented a bad omen. "I'll fix them, Captain," she said.

Aleksei nodded, then walked with Lilia toward the bunkers. Their mission had been a success, but the unpredictable and chaotic nature of the battle was unnerving. Nevertheless, more escort missions were to follow until they became routine, often without any challenge from enemy fighters. They would fly closer to the IL-2s and let the rear gunners play their role in the fight.

The regiment caught a break in the fighting for a day. Pilots were to be on alert, but no missions were planned. Lilia sat on the wing of her airplane, pen in hand, preparing to write a letter home. Fayina tended to various parts of the airplane, checking the tension of aileron cables and throttle adjustments. Lilia was surprised to see Aleksei walk down the lineup in his flight suit. "I didn't know we had a mission," she said.

"We don't. Replacement pilots have arrived." Aleksei answered, pointing to two men near the command bunker wearing flight suits. "I'm taking them up for training."

"What are you going to teach them?" Lilia asked.

"They each have two stars, just like you and Katya when you came to us. Maybe they have some talent. I'm going to make sure they have the skills." Aleksei replied.

Lilia and Fayina watched Aleksei and one of the replacement pilots taxi to the end of the runway and take off in a pair. The Yaks climbed higher, then moved through a routine of tight turns and rolls. They climbed higher still and practiced holding wing formation through rolls and dives. The advantage of the Yak-1 fighter was that it was lighter and had a tighter turn radius than most of the German aircraft they would face.

"He's really testing that new pilot." Fayina remarked, staring up at the sky.

"He has to get them ready if they're going to be flying with us." Lilia replied.

The two Yaks split apart in the air, then came back together in what appeared to be a mock dogfight, the sound of their engines roaring up and down. They moved through pitches and rolls until it was hard to tell which plane was which. Suddenly the sound of breaking, shearing metal clapped loudly across the airfield. The sound of only one engine remained buzzing in the sky. Lilia looked up to see one of the Yak's propeller locked in place. The airplane lost speed and began falling sideways, gaining more speed as it dropped. Over the edge of the runway, the Yak fighter plane continued its crippled and uncontrolled descent. With another loud clap it connected with the earth, into a pile of tangled wreckage.

"Oh, no!" Fayina cried out.

Lilia stared across the runway at the smoking wreckage.

The other Yak quickly landed and came to a stop. The canopy slung back, the pilot climbed out and took off his flight helmet. It was the replacement pilot Aleksei had been training. Pilots and ground crew quickly ran toward the wrecked airplane, Lilia followed. An ambulance drove toward the wreckage.

When Lilia reached the other side of the runway, ground crews were tearing at the cockpit, already having pulled off the canopy. They unfastened straps and pulled at the metal, attempting to extract the pilot. Four men pulled at the metal, bending the twisted frame, while another lifted the pilot out by his shoulders. They laid him down next the wrecked aircraft face up, his body crushed. Facing the sun, under his flight helmet, was the lifeless face of Aleksei. The grief left them silent but for a few sobs. They had lost their captain. Lilia felt the grief wash over her, closing her eyes as Fayina rushed to her side. It was the 19th of May, 1943.

A funeral service was arranged, and a casket was made. People from the local village of Pavlovka had gathered flowers and prepared a proper gravesite. The ceremony was held two days later. A low fog had descended over the ceremony. Aleksei's casket lay before pilots and ground crew of the 73rd Guards. They stood in a semi-circle, with Lilia in the center, amidst the fog. Each took their turn placing flowers on the casket then stepping back in line. Lilia laid down a handful of flowers herself and stepped back to stare at the casket. The other pilots quietly pulled their pistols and aimed them at the sky. At Sasha's nod, they pulled the triggers and rang out a gun salute to their fallen comrade.

Lilia and Aleksei had known each other only four months, from a winter into spring. Yet in that time, his heart had turned. Aleksei Frolovich Solomatin did not leave the world as a cynic. He left it as a man in love.

Chapter 13

Lilia was morose after the death of Aleksei. Colonel Golyshev had noticed it and was reluctant to put her back on combat duty. Lilia hadn't realized herself how deeply she had felt for Aleksei until after he was gone, lamenting to her mother in a letter home that she would likely never meet someone like him again. Katya had also observed the change and pulled her aside. "Your Aleksei died a hero," Katya said to her. Lilia merely nodded. "Let's have a meal." Katya continued, then called out. "Fayina, come and join us for lunch."

Fayina set down her tools and walked over to join them. "Ina," she said. "Please call me Ina. That's my name."

"Ina." Katya repeated. "Very well, then."

Katya sat between Lilia and Ina in the canteen and began to sing a song from the region of her hometown, *Old Dnieper*, softly at first, then more robustly. Pilots from the next table joined in as the rest of the bunker listened quietly. Katya put her arms over Lilia and Ina's shoulders as she sang. Pilots clapped softly as she finished. It was the best she could do to give comfort, yet the only form of comfort Lilia desired was to be back in the air. She would be, ten days after Aleksei's funeral.

On the 31st of May, 1943, a situation had developed on the front line. The German Army had deployed an observation balloon and were using it to direct their artillery fire with brutal effectiveness. Taking down the balloon had become the number one priority on the southern frontline. By mid-afternoon four pilots had already been lost. In the last attempt, a pilot was lost while his wingman barely survived. He had returned to base in his shredded airplane, landing on only one wheel. After pulling himself out of his crippled aircraft, he briefed the colonel on the ground.

"He was hit by the eighty-eights. Nothing is getting past them." The pilot said in anguish, referring to the German Army's eighty-eight millimeter anti-aircraft guns.

Lilia had overheard, having closely followed the day's events. She watched as Golyshev, frustrated and feeling the low state of morale amongst the pilots, retreated to the command bunker with a look of torment on his face. Lilia turned to Ina, standing next to her airplane. "Have the cannon loaded with incendiary rounds," Lilia ordered then walked toward the command bunker. She entered the bunker to find Golyshev alone, pacing back and forth. "Show me where the balloon is, on the map," Lilia demanded.

Golyshev turned to face her, seeing the seriousness of her expression. "I'll shoot it down. Just show me where to find it," she continued.

Golyshev paused a moment, then walked to a table with a map of the frontline spread across it. He looked at Lilia again, then put his finger to a spot on the map and tapped it twice. Lilia nodded and left the bunker.

Ten minutes later Lilia was in the air, speeding west towards the frontline, her fighter plane fully armed and fueled. She spotted the balloon at altitude from twenty kilometers out, on a direct course. She dropped altitude to less than one hundred meters then flew lower still. She banked hard right, flying parallel to the front line as it turned from open fields and trenches to hillsides and growths of trees to her left. Lilia turned again, banking hard left to fly straight across the line, pushing full throttle just above the treetops. Across the enemy line, Lilia climbed again. She turned her airplane slowly to the left to put herself at altitude, directly west of the balloon.

Putting the late afternoon sun directly behind her, Lilia dove at the observation balloon, unseen. Flying out of the sun, she let loose a steady barrage of incendiary cannon rounds. The balloon caught fire and began to fall. Flames overtook it as she continued to fire. At the end of her attack run, Lilia could see men tumbling out of the observation platform below the flaming cloth above them. She banked hard left again, avoiding the range of the eighty-eights, and retraced her path back across the frontline and returned to base. After the success of her mission, news of her tactic spread quickly across the southern front.

Several more balloons were shot down elsewhere on the frontline using the same tactic. Destroying the observation balloons had brought the frontline back to stasis. It had taken away the German Army's advantage in the ground war, and caused them to seek a new advantage in the air war.

Two weeks later, on the 16th of June, the radio operators called out enemy aircraft spotted deep behind the line. Lilia and Colonel Golyshev answered the call, flying as a pair to make the intercept. They flew to the area south of where the aircraft had been spotted, and climbed in altitude to search the sky below.

"They should be here." Golyshev said over the radio, while looking in all directions.

Lilia held to his wing as they flew a large circle. As they rounded a full circle, a dark speck appeared in the distance before them. "I see something, two o'clock," she called out.

Golyshev straightened course to fly directly at the dark spec in the distance, growing larger as they approached. Before they could discern the type of aircraft approaching them, it rolled over and dove to make its escape, revealing its twin engine, twin boom design. The rectangular frame and glass encased cockpit for a three-person crew was that of the Focke Wulf 189 reconnaissance aircraft. Nicknamed "The Owl," it was the eyes of the Luftwaffe.

"Should we chase it?" Lilia asked.

"No. Escort! Twelve o'clock." Golyshev replied as four Messerschmitt 109s appeared before them.

Golyshev and Lilia climbed to meet the Messerschmitts, bullets spraying across the sky between them. The gap closing quickly, a bullet ripped through Goylshev's cockpit, piercing schrapnel into his left shoulder. The two Yaks flew through the pack of Messerschmitts, flashing by, canopy to canopy.

"I'm hit! Break it off! Break it off!" He ordered.

"Return to base, Colonel. I'll hold them off." Lilia replied.

Golyshev dove away, fighting the pain from his shoulder, making his escape to the east. Meanwhile, the Owl made its escape to the west. Lilia banked hard right to re-engage the Messerschmitts. She flew between them in tight turns, exploiting the logistics of four fighters against one with the Yak's tighter turn radius. She blasted her guns across their wings in quick passes while they tried not to shoot each other.

Golyshev returned to base and landed. He called for help and the ground crew helped him out of his airplane. The medic was summoned and quickly tended to his wounded shoulder, making efforts to first stop the bleeding. Golyshev watched the sky all the while, knowing that if Lilia had not turned to face the Messers again, they might have quickly caught up and finished him. After a few minutes passed, he heard the sound of a Klimov engine in the distance. As it came closer, he was relieved to see that it was Lilia. Her airplane glided in low, her landing gear still folded under the wings. The propeller dug into the runway as the belly of her airplane touched down and skidded sideways to a stop. The canopy slid back and Lilia climbed out of her airplane, bullet holes visible on the fuselage and wings.

Lilia had held off the four fighters, exchanging bursts for several minutes, until they could not continue. They had been far behind the line and their mission to protect the Owl was already complete. They had dived away all at once, pulled into formation and turned full speed toward to the west.

After the sighting of the Owl, more than a month passed in relative calm. In the second week of July, 1943, Katya and Lilia stood by the lineup awaiting orders. Katya stared at the sky to the west. "We've seen this before." Katya said calmly. "There hasn't been a major offensive in almost a month."

"They've given us some rest." Lilia replied.

"They're preparing for something big. They have to give it everything now. They only want to fight us when they have us outnumbered" said Katya. "We'll be fighting against a mob."

"More of them to shoot at." Lilia answered.

Katya smiled. "They may beat us with numbers, but we'll be sure to make it cost them, and maybe we'll die as heroes." Katya replied.

While the ground war raged on, the Germans had gathered resources for another operation. Though they had suffered terrible losses, it would only cause them to persist in the blitzkreig strategy that had previously brought them the most success. The next blitz arrived on the 16th of July. The Radio Operators called out what the spotters had seen crossing the line, a massive formation of bombers and fighters, along with their location and heading. Golyshev quickly ordered a flight of six Yaks up to meet them. When they spotted the formation approaching it appeared like a swarm of birds, thirty Junckers 88 bombers, with an escort of eight Messerschmitt 109s. Flying at altitude above the bombers, Golyshev gave the order. "Attack!" he shouted. There was no other instruction. It was six against thirty-eight.

Lilia dove straight into the storm, firing cannon rounds at a bomber's engines. They lit on fire, trailing smoke. The bomber's left wing split off. The careening mass dropped out of the formation in flames. The Yaks split into pairs, making another pass through the bomber formation before their escort of eight Messerschmitts dove on them. Lilia turned to take aim at a Messerschmitt joining the fight, raking the fuselage with machine gun fire before its engine blew. Smoke billowed from the engine as it dove away.

Golyshev struggled to shake the three Messerschmitts that had all focused their attention on him, while Katya, and Sasha flew as a pair, still raking the engines of the bomber formation.

Another Messerschmitt fired at Lilia amidst the chaos. She felt the sting of shrapnel hit her right hand. She turned to aim at the Messer and fired, putting holes in the tail section. Another Messerschmitt fired on Lilia, killing her engine.

With her engine dead, Lilia nosed her aircraft down into a glide, a passing Messerschmitt firing on her again, ripping holes in her wing. Lilia continued her descent, finally leveling out to land wheels up in a field, skidding to a stop. Golyshev suffered a similar fate several hundred meters away.

A Red Army truck, with half a dozen soldiers on foot found Lilia next to her downed aircraft holding her bleeding right hand. A soldier paused a moment, surprised that the downed pilot they had found was a woman, then noticed her injury. "We'll get you to a hospital." The soldier told her.

"No." Lilia answered. "No hospital. It isn't serious enough. I need to get back to my base."

"Please, let us get you to a medic first." The Soldier replied. "He'll wrap it for you." Lilia nodded in agreement, reluctantly.

Lilia's airplane was returned to base and repairs begun immediately as the Luftwaffe attacks would only persist. Their main objective had changed once again to prioritize taking the city of Kursk to the north. The fury and chaos of the Eastern front was building to its most dramatic and decisive of the war. The formations of Luftwaffe bombers and fighters they had seen near Rostov were to serve as the southern tip of a pincer movement around Kursk. Over the city of Kursk itself, air battles were raging daily with as many as one thousand aircraft in the air at once.

Three days after she was shot down, with her right hand tightly bandaged, Lilia was flying escort duty with Katya Budanova. They met up with and settled into a high cover position over a formation of IL-2s as they roared across the line. The Shturmoviks soon found their target and attacked in figure eights while Lilia and Katya flew cover in a circle above them. The IL-2s had nearly completed their attack on the ground targets when the Messerschmitts arrived. Lilia had spotted them to the east well before they could attack, making their run straight at the bombers.

"Going in," Lilia called over the radio, aiming her fighter plane to intercept.

Katya held tightly to Lilia's wing as they dove to make the pass on the eight Messerschmitts. Before the enemy fighters could open their guns on the bombers, Lilia and Katya were firing at the lead fighters, forcing them to break off their attack.

The IL-2s finished their run and turned to fly back across the line as Lilia and Katya held off the enemy fighters. Outnumbered once again, the Messerschmitts maneuvered to use their number to their advantage. Lilia quickly downed a Messerschmitt, blasting cannon rounds at a pair, setting one of their engines on fire. Katya had broken off to engage four of the remaining fighters by herself. Amidst the confusion, Katya put her guns on one of the Messerschmitts, exploding its gas tank. It dropped away in flames. Katya had earned her final star, as one of the remaining three turned to put her in his sights. The bullets pierced the nose of Katya's airplane, wrecking her engine. The oil pressure gauge dropped to zero as smoke engulfed the airplane. Another burst of gunfire pierced the cockpit, bullets tearing into her chest.

The remaining fighters broke off the fight as Katya made her descent.

"I'm hit!" Katya called out over the radio. "I've got no oil pressure. I have to put it down," she relayed in anguish.

Lilia watched helpless from her cockpit as Katya neared the rough ground below. Her fighter plane bounced on a hard landing, then dropped into a bomb crater in a violent stop.

"Katya!" Lilia called out. There was no reply. Katya Budanova died in her cockpit. Her lacerated body expired before local villagers could reach her airplane to pull her out. Lilia returned to base alone. It was the 19th of July, 1943.

Lilia landed her airplane and taxied into the lineup. Ina was waiting with her tool cart. As the propeller came to a stop, she put blocks under the wheels. The canopy slid back and Lilia climbed out and stepped down from the wing.

"Where is Katya?" Ina asked.

"Katya is not coming back," Lilia replied somberly.

The sadness registered on Ina's face, but she found no words.

"Paint another star on the plane," said Lilia then walked toward Colonel Golyshev, standing outside the command bunker with Sasha. Ina watched as they huddled together and Lilia delivered the bad news. Lilia then pulled out her pistol, aimed it at the sky, and fired a single shot for her fallen comrade.

The loss of Katya Budanova was a difficult blow to the morale of the 73rd Guards, but there was little time to mourn. Two days later Lilia was in a flight of four Yaks on Golyshev's wing when they met a flight of twelve Messerschmitt 109s.

They quickly scattered into a chaotic scramble. With four Messerschmitts on her tail, Lilia flipped her airplane into a tight barrel roll, and skidded, dropping behind the pack as they flew past her. She put her guns on a Messerschmitt, and pressed the trigger, blasting machine gun rounds across the fuselage. Flames poured from the midsection, then erupted in a fireball. The remaining three enemy fighters split, banking in opposite directions to spread out and turn for a new attack. As Lilia chased a single Messerschmitt, the other two closed on her six. As she broke right to evade their guns, machine gun rounds punched through the top of her airplane's nose. Smoke poured out as she dove away from the fight.

"I'm hit!" Lilia called out over the radio over the frantic voices, each outnumbered in their own fight. Lilia shut off the fuel supply, bringing the smoke to an end. The propeller slowed to a stop as she glided in for a landing in a field below. The airplane went silent until it hit the field with a thud and skidded to a stop.

By the end of July, 1943, the fury and chaos of the Eastern Front had built to a crescendo. Back in Moscow, action reports from the frontline came in faster than the general staff could read them, yet a detailed account of Lilia's downing of the observation balloon three weeks prior had landed on the desk Colonel Zuchenko. He had ordered an article written, and an artist's depiction to be drawn. Pleased with both, he was preparing to have it printed and circulated across the front line when his Aide Grigor entered his office carrying a file folder and a deeply worried look on his face. Zuchenko paused at Grigor's expression.

"What is it?" Zuchenko demanded.

"Something you need to see." Grigor replied, setting the file on the desk. "This was discovered in the archive," he explained nervously.

Colonel Zuchenko opened the file to study what contained records of the arrest, trial, and execution of Lilia's father. Colonel Zuchenko froze as he took in the information.

Vladimir Litvyak. Declared an Enemy of the People.

Executed at Lubyanka Prison. Wife, Anna. Son, Yuri.

Daughter... Lilia.

Colonel Zuchenko was gripped by panic at the realization. He had unwittingly raised someone officially classified as a traitor near to the status of a hero. Nothing could be allowed to interfere in any way with the perception of the infallibility of the state. To be uncovered as the architect of such an incongruity with the official position could cost him his life.

"Does anyone else know about this?" Zuchenko asked quietly.

"No, I found it myself." Grigor answered.

"Good. Good. We can fix this." Zuchenko replied, trying to calm himself. "We have to fix this."

"How do we do that?" Grigor asked.

"I'll prepare the documents. You get the car ready."

"Ready for what?" asked Grigor.

"A very long drive." Zuchenko answered. "We need to pay our Lilia a visit."

Grigor nodded and walked out the door.

Chapter 14

Colonel Zuchenko sat in the back seat of the black sedan, driven by Grigor, through the outskirts of Moscow to a series of country roads. It crossed through farmlands, rolling hills, and for a time through a forest with trees that reminded him of his childhood in Siberia and of life in the Taiga.

As a boy, Stanislav Zuchenko lived in a cabin in the forest with his father and his younger brother, Ivan. The winters of his youth were bitterly cold, all evidence of life hidden beneath the ice and snow. Though the struggle to survive in the Taiga pushed them against nature's extremes, his father told him many times to work hard and trust that God would provide. When the spring would arrive once again, the ice would crack and melt, the landscape turned green and burst forth the abundance of creation. Rivers swelled from the melting snow, teeming with fish. There were berries to be picked, and garden beds to be planted. The summers stretched into autumn in the never-ending preparation for the next coming winter. There were vegetables to be pickled and fish to be smoked, potatoes, carrots and beets to be stored, and piles of wood to be chopped and stacked. Before the first freeze he would stand on the bank of a river in the evenings, fishing deep into the twilight with his younger brother, hoping for the last catch of the season.

In the winter of 1911, Stanislav was twelve years old. His brother Ivan was eight. After an exceptionally long and cold winter, yet another storm extending it further into spring, their provisions had run out. Their traps laid for small game were empty, their stores of potatoes and carrots cooked for the last bowls of soup. Suffering hunger while awaiting the melt, Stanislav, his father and brother harnessed their three horses to the sledge to travel to the nearest town in the hopes of trading pelts for food.

The sledge glided over the snow, making fresh tracks as the horses held a steady pace. The air still bitter cold, turned the horses' breath to white mist. After several miles they reached a crossroads. Stanislav's father parked the sledge and tied up the horses. An old man and an old woman held open the trading post through the winter to trade furs for food and supplies. The old woman saw the gaunt complexion of his sons faces and beckoned them inside. She poured bowls of hot beet soup for him and his sons and set them on a table, then urged them to sit.

"Please, sit, eat." She spoke patiently.

"Thank you." The elder Zuchenko replied. "We've run very low on supplies."

"This winter is testing us all," said the old woman.

Stanislav and his brother looked to their father for guidance.

"Eat boys, eat." He told them.

After they had finished their bowls of soup, the elder Zuchenko pulled out a pouch and laid several small furs on the table. The old woman ran her fingers through their soft fine fur.

"Yes, these will do." She said, knowing they would likely end up as hats or gloves in a fancy shop in Moscow or St. Petersberg.

The exchange would provide them enough potatoes and grain to survive well into the spring. Stanislav helped his father load the sacks onto the sledge before untying the horses. "The ice will melt soon, and we'll have fish again." Stanislav's father said to him as he turned the sledge and horses back onto the road.

They traveled through the forest at a steady rate. Stanislav's father Boris urged the horses to run faster to reach their home with daylight to spare for restocking their provisions. The lengthy and brutal winter had not only left them hungry, so too the wolves. They heard the howls of the pack echo through the trees before they saw the flash of a grey shadow running in parallel to them. Stanislav's father whipped the horses again, sensing the danger. There were more grey shadows and the sounds of howling converging around them. An instant later, the grey shadows spilled out of the trees surrounding them. Two-dozen ravenous wolves converged around the sledge, snarling and nipping at the horses. Boris whipped the horses into full speed as the wolves growled and bared their teeth. Young Stanislav and his brother Ivan sat paralyzed in fear as the wolves pressed their attack.

The horses collided with each other as the wolves bit at their sides. The horses balked and reared. Stanislav's father whipped them again, setting them forward through the pack. Yet the wolves would not relent. The elder Zuchenko looked back to see Stanislav and his brother staring out the back of the sledge with a cold expression on his face. He reached back and picked up Ivan up by his belt and tossed him over the back of the sledge.

Stanislav looked on in horror as the wolves ripped into his brother who let out a final scream that turned to silence before his blood could turn the snow red. With their attention diverted, the wolves stopped chasing. Stanislav stared back in shock, then to his father who continued to furiously whip the horses. It was the sort of nightmare one reads about only in fairy tales, yet he had seen it with his own eyes.

Neither the younger, nor the elder Zuchenko spoke for several hours. They returned to the cabin in silence, unloaded the sacks and stored them. They unbridled the horses and returned them to the barn with hay to eat. Stanislav and his father stewed potatoes for supper. Stanislav said not a word, but cried continuously in a gentle whimper until his father could stand no more.

"Enough. Enough tears," he demanded. "I did what had to be done. They would have eaten us all." He explained.

Stanislav turned to his father, an unsatisfied look on his face. "I hope you must never make such a decision. I sacrificed my youngest son so my oldest may live. Your brother died so you could live. Pray for him, Slava. Pray for his soul in heaven." He pleaded. "When it is my time, I will face God and ask forgiveness. That is all I can do."

The boy stared at his father, incredulous. "There is no god," he replied.

The spring of 1911 broke through and filled the Taiga with life again, but for Stanislav Zuchenko the world had changed forever. The wolves would haunt his nightmares, to remind him nightly that the world was cruel and unforgiving. In the years that followed, he yearned for something more than a life in the Taiga. One summer he caught a glimpse of it. A mining exploration company was passing through his village, and on their carriage he saw a strange object in the dark of night. It was a fire that burned without fire. He marveled at the sight of it, an electric light bulb.

"Is it magic?" He asked of a miner.

"No, it's the future." The man replied.

Later that summer Stanislav Zuchenko would read the literature of the Bolsheviks and imagine the something more. Somewhere beyond the glow of an electric light bulb was the promise of a technological utopia where machines would ease the burdens of men. The Bolsheviks spoke of a future where everyone had an equal share. What stood in their way were the decadences of the Tsars, their magnificent palaces and bottomless wealth. He would join the revolution, considering it nothing less than the right of the people to participate in the modern world. It would leave him with a battlefield injury, and after it a secret addiction to morphine. He would also achieve the rank of Colonel in the NKVD.

The murder of the Tsars and their children and ministers in 1917 was only the beginning. They had succeeded in throwing off the old order, yet the work that lay before them was to establish the socialist society that was to come after it, and maintain complete and total control over it. The real revolution would continue indefinitely. The promised utopia of a younger Stanislav Zuchenko, imagined somewhere beyond the electric light bulb, could only be achieved with the blunt tools of collectivization. While the party fractured with internal struggles, Colonel Zuchenko carried out his assignments as they were handed to him by the party's inner circle. They were the ongoing implementations of one executive order after another, from land reforms and the creation of collective farms, the murder of Kulak farmers, followed by crop failures and food shortages, to constant political purges and mass arrests. While the failures of the system had arisen from the very beginning, the revolution devolved further into casual, often sadistic brutality, coercion, torture, executions, and assassinations. For tens of millions of Russians, the revolution would bring the full measure of horror, debasement, and death, all in service to the dream of a socialist utopia for which the ends justified any means.

In the summer of 1943, Colonel Zuchenko's work had brought him to the airbase of the 73rd Guards. The black sedan crept slowly down a dirt road towards the runway and bunkers. Grigor parked the car by the side of the runway. Colonel Zuchenko stepped out of the back seat carrying a leather satchel. It was quiet. There were only three fighter planes parked in the lineup. The mechanics and armorers barely looked up to notice him as they went about their work. The NKVD Colonel approached an armorer as he pushed a cart of ammunition toward one of the airplanes.

"Where is the Colonel of this regiment?"

The armorer pointed to the sky. "On a mission," he replied.

"What about Lieutenant Litvyak?" Zuchenko pressed.

"Also on a mission." The armorer answered.

Colonel Zuchenko stood by the edge of the runway patiently, holding his satchel until the silence was broken by the sound of Klimov engines buzzing in the distance. The roar of the engines grew louder as they approached. Several Yak fighter planes landed in succession, Lilia's among them. Zuchenko spotted the painted white lily on the fuselage as Lilia pulled her fighter plane into the lineup. Next to the white lily, there were eleven small red stars. Colonel Zuchenko had been comfortable in an office in Moscow while she had earned them all. The canopy slung back and Lilia climbed out. Ina handed her a cane as she stepped down from the wing. She took it in her left hand, her right hand wrapped tightly in bandages stained with blood.

Golyshev climbed out of his airplane and yelled down the line. "Get them refueled and ready! We're up again in twenty minutes," he shouted then walked quickly to the command bunker, passing Colonel Zuchenko without a word spoken.

Lilia took off her flight helmet and shook her blonde hair in the wind, then followed Golyshev, walking with a cane and a slight limp. She didn't notice the NKVD Colonel until he stepped in front of her path.

"Lieutenant Litvyak, we meet again."

Lilia looked up and stopped, recognizing the uniform, and then the man.

"Hello, Colonel," she answered.

"You've been injured," said Zuchenko, noticing the bandages on her right hand.

"It's not serious." Lilia replied.

"It seems you have had quite a lot of success on the frontline." He said, motioning to the small red stars on her airplane.

"I'm only doing my part." Lilia replied.

"Yet so much more," he answered. "You are an inspiration to our soldiers all across the front, and to our workers in the factories."

"Is that so?" Lilia asked.

"Yes, it is."

"Have you come all this way from Moscow, Colonel?"

"Yes," he replied.

"To speak with me?" Lilia asked.

"We have a small problem," he replied.

"You drove here from Moscow for a small problem?" she asked.

"Certain information has come to light, about your father." Zuchenko answered.

"What is the problem?" Lilia asked directly.

"It betrays appearances. Certainly you can understand."

"My father was innocent. He committed no crime." Lilia answered.

"I cannot change what is done. We all have orders. They must be followed or the system will fail. There cannot be exceptions." He spoke softly. "What I ask is merely a formality."

"What is it you ask, Colonel?" Lilia replied.

Colonel Zuchenko fumbled to open his satchel and retrieve a piece of paper. "Your signature, that is all. Sign this and our problem goes away." He said as he held the sheet of paper in front of her.

"What does it say?" Lilia asked, staring at the page.

"That you renounce him," he answered.

Lilia stared at the Colonel. He had imagined he could intimidate her, an attempt to elicit the one emotion she could no longer feel, fear. Suddenly he felt it himself. Could he arrest her and escape with his life? He had a pistol on his waist, but so did she. So did every pilot at the base. He began to sense their eyes upon him in sideways glances as he held the paper before her. Would he keep his own life if he failed?

"It's only a signature, a formality. It's all I ask." He pleaded.

"You ask that I forsake my father, betray his name and my own." Lilia answered.

"It's only a signature, Lieutenant, a formality," Zuchenko pleaded again.

"I have another mission, Colonel. You'll have to excuse me." Lilia said, then continued toward the command bunker.

"I must have it today." Zuchenko called out behind her.

Fifteen minutes later, Lilia sat in her cockpit. Ina called up to her.

"It's fueled and armed, Lilia. Ready for flight."

"Ina, come up." Lilia answered.

Ina climbed up on the wing. "What is it?" She asked.

Lilia handed her a pen and a piece of paper.

"I want to write a letter to my mother, but I can't hold the pen. Could you write it for me?" Lilia asked.

"Of course," said Ina, taking the pen and paper. She sat on the wing ready to take dictation.

"My dearest Mamushka, it is difficult to find even a brief moment to write, to tell you that I am alive and well, and that I love you. I long for the time when I may return to you, and live a peaceful, happy life. I want to tell you of everything I've lived through and felt while we were apart..." Lilia spoke as Ina scribbled the words.

Colonel Zuchenko leaned against the black sedan nearby, watching Lilia as he smoked a cigarette, contemplating his next move. He had once imagined Lilia to be like a sister he had never had.

"...In my dream, I stand on the bank of a fast rushing river. My love waves to me from the other side. When I wake, the war goes on, and I fear it has swallowed me completely. I must say goodbye for now and return to the fighting. Love and kisses, Your Lilia." She concluded.

"I'll mail it for you," said Ina, folding the page in half.

The formation of six Yak fighters was airborne minutes later, en route to fly escort for a squadron of Shturmoviks. They found the squadron and pulled into a high cover position before crossing the line. The Shturmoviks found their target, a row of Panzer tanks followed by soldiers on foot marching to reinforce the line and push across the Donets River south of the city of Kharkov. The Shturmoviks dropped their bombs, flying figure eights over the formation, blowing up the lead tank and scattering the soldiers on foot. The Yaks maintained high cover, flying circles with no resistance until the Shturmoviks completed their mission and pulled back into formation. Tall clouds filled the sky as they turned back toward the line.

A pack of Messerschmitt 109s dove out of high cloud cover to surprise the formation of Yak fighters. Once again, they were outnumbered. After three bullets hit her fuselage, Lilia kicked the pedals and pulled the stick, breaking from her formation to face them head on. The formation of Yaks were quickly split apart, each engaging multiple Messerschmitts on their own. Lilia was facing five against one amidst the towering clouds. She flipped her aircraft in a series of rolls to put her gun sights on one of the Messers, while keeping the rest off of her six o'clock. In a fast pass, she delivered a stream of bullets to light a Messerschmitt on fire. It dove away in flames while the remaining four coordinated their attack. Bullets ripped into the nose of Lilia's fighter plane. A whisper of black smoke streamed out, then poured from her engine, suddenly losing power. As the throttle began to sputter, Lilia steered toward a tall cloud. With flames spitting from the engine cowling, her fighter plane trailing black smoke, and bullets streaking past her, Lilia plunged into the tall cloud, cloaking her airplane in its white mist. She pulled back the throttle and watched the propeller slow to a dead spin. She slung back the canopy and smelled the smoke as it rushed through the slipstream. She unbuckled her seatbelt and checked her parachute harness. Lilia steadied herself against the edge of the cockpit then jammed the stick forward. The airplane nosed down, vaulting her into the abyss. The Messers screamed past above her as she hurled through the mist. She dropped out of the cloud to find herself plummeting toward the ground below. She pulled a cord, letting loose her parachute to catch the air. It popped open to leave her dangling, drifting slowly back to Earth.

At the airbase, Colonel Zuchenko stood by the edge of the runway awaiting Lilia's return. He watched as the Yaks appeared in the sky and finally touched down and pulled into the lineup. Of the six that had taken off, only five returned. Lilia was not among them. The accounts of her last battle were varied. They had been split up and lost sight of her in the clouds. One had seen her down a Messer, while another had seen smoke from her engine.

They all stood together watching the sky in the hope that Lilia would return, but as the minutes passed it was increasingly unlikely, and ultimately impossible as she would be out of fuel. Lilia Litvyak never returned to her base. It was the 1st of August, 1943, the day she disappeared in the skies above the front.

Colonel Zuchenko returned to the back seat of the black sedan. Grigor sat in the driver's seat. He looked back at the Colonel in the rear view mirror.

"What now?" Grigor asked.

"We return to Moscow. We continue our work." Colonel Zuchenko replied.

Grigor started the car, then turned back to ask a question. "What about Lieutenant Litvyak?"

The Colonel stared at him coldly for a moment, before answering. "She will be erased from history."

Chapter 15

Less than a year after Lilia disappeared in the skies above the front, the American and Allied forces entered the European theater of war, landing on the beaches of France. The Red Army would continue its fight, pushing slowly across the eastern front, ever closer to Germany. The Allied powers would fight through the fields of France and the Ardennes Forest, pushing east. In May of 1945, the Nazi high command surrendered as the Allies and the Red Army converged on the east and west sides of Berlin, finally bringing the war to an end. Camps were liberated, freeing millions of the prisoners of war that had survived. They would trickle back to their home countries in the years that followed. Lilia Litvyak was not amongst them.

After the war, the rebuilding could begin. The pieces of a scorched and shattered landscape were slowly put back together, and in the aftermath the histories could be written. Upon his return to the Soviet Union, it was reported by another pilot that Lilia had been seen in a camp. When she failed to return after the war, the accusations arose. Despite her deeds, in the final postwar accounting, Lilia was considered a suspected traitor in the eyes of the state.

Lilia's brother Yuri would never see his sister again, nor Anna her daughter. Though still merely a teenager, Yuri Litvyak's problems had only begun. His father caught up in the purge and executed as an "Enemy of the State," and his sister considered a possible traitor, Yuri was given the status of a "non-person" within Soviet society. He would find it difficult to find and keep various jobs, though he would insist that his sister was a hero and not a traitor. The pressure from government officials would always return in attempts to silence his inconvenient stories that conflicted with the official narrative of the infallible Soviet state. He had even tried to change his last name to that of his mother's maiden name. Unless Lilia's body could be found to prove she had been killed in the war, her status would remain.

Ina found Anna and Yuri after returning to her own hometown of Moscow, and would visit them often. Hearing of Yuri's ongoing political problems, Ina had vowed to search for Lilia's body until she was found. In the summers, she would travel to the Donbass to search the countryside for Lilia's remains, and tell Lilia's story. All the while, the legend of Lilia Litvyak, the courageous fighter pilot, grew. Though Yuri's problems persisted, as long as Ina continued her search and continued to tell Lilia's story, and insist that her body would be found, there was hope.

By the late summer of 1979, it had been 36 years since Lilia Litvyak had taken off in her Yakovlev fighter plane and not returned to her airbase. It had been confirmed by fellow pilots that Lilia was shot down behind the enemy line, yet neither her body nor her aircraft were found. Ina had since met the man she would marry after the war and took his surname. He would join her in the search for Lilia. Along with her husband, Ina Pasportnikova, would spend her summers searching for Lilia's aircraft and remains. In their search, they had discovered the wreckage of almost 90 aircraft and the bodies of dozens of pilots who could finally be given a proper burial. Ina enjoyed the long walks across the open fields of the Donbass, hearing the sounds of birds and insects and wind through the grass. Yet the recollections lingered of what it looked and sounded like during the war, bomb craters, destroyed tanks, the thumping of artillery percussions, and the rattle of machine guns somewhere in the distance, and the terrifying screech of Katyusha rockets.

Ina's stories about Lilia, the blonde haired pilot only five feet tall with blue-grey eyes that had done battle in the skies above, had inspired the locals to aid in her search. Two dozen Young Pioneers, dressed in blue shorts, white shirts, and red scarves had turned out that day, following Ina as they fanned out across the fields to search for Lilia and listen to the stories of her exploits during the war.

As Ina continued her search, she told of Lilia's story year after year, yet the Soviet government still would not award Lilia its highest honor, the title of Hero of the Soviet Union.

Petitions had been made at the highest levels, but the petitions were repeatedly refused. Rumors had persisted since her disappearance that Lilia had parachuted safely to the ground and been taken prisoner, and even that her voice had been heard over German radio.

On a clear day in August of that year, Ina discovered another airplane. Within a thicket of overgrown vines, under the blue sky of the Donbass, peaked out the tip of a tailfin resembling in shape that of a Yak-1 fighter plane. Children from the local chapter of The Young Pioneers that had turned out to help that day quickly went to work to uncover the downed airplane. They cut their way through the vines to reveal the tailfin, left to the elements for decades, and continued until the fuselage saw sunlight once again. The work continued throughout the morning hours until finally the cockpit was uncovered. A boy of ten years old pulled back more vines to stand on the wing of the airplane, rubbing on the perspex cockpit attempting to peer inside. In the dusty light he could just make out a figure inside, seated and slumped over.

"There's someone in there," the boy said aloud. He rubbed the cockpit further and put his hand up to look again.

"Is it Lilia?" Another child asked.

"I don't think so." He answered.

Ina stepped up to the fuselage and brushed away the dirt until a number 34 in white was revealed, and next to it the small painted image of a tiger. She stepped back knowing what she had found. It was Mikhail. The local authorities were informed of their find. The airplane was excavated and Mikhail's body was prepared for a proper burial.

Ina and her husband retired in the evening to the country cottage from which they staged their searches of the Donbass. Ina's husband stood over maps laid out on the kitchen table, marked with notes of the areas they had searched and of the finds they had made. "Where should we search tomorrow?" He asked. Ina sat silent in an armchair as he studied the map further, laying a finger down on it. "We haven't searched here." He continued.

"We can stop looking for Lilia now." Ina replied. "We're not going to find her."

"You want to give up?" He asked.

"No. We won't find her because she survived."

"What?"

"Another pilot was with her in the camp. He knew her when she was in the 9th Guards. He told me himself." Ina explained. "Lilia was captured, and she couldn't come home."

Ina's husband paused, perplexed. He slumped into an armchair next to her. "Who have we been searching for all this time?" Asked Ina's husband.

"The pilot we found today." Ina's husband listened quietly as she confessed.

When the war came to an end in 1945, Ina returned home to Moscow. She had attended victory parades in her cleaned and pressed uniform, wearing her various medals proudly. But the war had taken a heavy toll, and the work of returning to something of a normal life had just begun. Questions had to be answered of loved ones not returned. In those post war days she took a trip to the remote village Mikhail had told her about. She walked into the village as a stranger. It was a small affair, dirt roads and thatched roof homes, with small garden plots and livestock. With the faded black and white photo Mikhail had given her for safekeeping in hand, she searched the village to find his family's home, the one in the picture with his mother standing in front. After determining a match she summoned the courage to knock on the front door. Ina was greeted by his mother and his sisters and welcomed inside. They laughed and cried and shared stories. Although Ina had lost her lover in the war, it was as though she had gained another mother and two sisters, and to them she had made a solemn promise, she would find Mikhail. Not wanting to tell her husband the true intent of her search, she had told everyone that her search had been for Lilia out of convenience. Yet her real intent had always been to find the remains of the pilot she had loved and lost to the war, the one who had first called her Ina.

"I told a lie so I could keep a promise." Ina explained to her husband in the darkening evening in the cottage. "I have kept that promise."

Ina's husband thought of all the planes and pilots they had recovered, and the closure they had given to so many families in the work they had done. Their summers in the Donbass had only strengthened the bond between them and given them both a sense of purpose in putting the pieces of their war ravaged nation back together. It had given them a shared and noble quest, that Lilia would be remembered with the title of Hero.

Ina's husband sat back in his chair and asked, "What about Lilia?"

"She got away." Ina replied.

"She was a hero, wasn't she?" He answered.

"She was."

"She should be remembered as such." He replied.

"How?" Ina asked.

In 1979, another petition was made to the Soviet state, with the claim that the pieces of her airplane and the remains of her body had been found. When Soviet officials demanded to examine the body, it was not produced and the petition was met with another official rejection. While the Soviet state had refused to grant Lilia the title of Hero, Ina continued to tell her story, and in so doing she had ignited brushfires in the hearts of the Russian people, stoking their desire to see that Lilia be given their nation's highest honor. There were magazine and newspaper articles, and books written about her. A school was named in Lilia's honor. A museum for Lilia had also been commissioned, with letters and memorabilia donated by Anna Litvyak. A monument was also erected with the help of a sculptor and an architect in front of the school that bore Lilia's name. It showed the fierce expression of the pilot who had once defended the skies above. It stands today in the small coal mining town of Krasnyi Luch, in the Donbass, in what is now the Ukraine. By the continued telling of her story, Lilia Litvyak had become a legend, and her story had become a living thing. The Soviet state and the Russian people were at a stalemate. The Soviet state was unable to prove Lilia had been captured, and without her body, it was not possible to prove she had been killed in combat.

In 1982, another discovery was made, further north in the Orel region. Beneath thickets of overgrown vines and brush, a Yak-1 fighter plane was found. Inside was the diminutive figure of its female pilot, still in her flight suit, having perished in her cockpit. It was the remains of Antonina Lebedeva. She had played her part in the war and had also disappeared in the skies above the front. On the 10th of January, 1943, Antonina downed a Messerschmitt 109 to earn a single star. On the 17th of July, 1943, Antonina flew out from her airbase to the Battle of Kursk. Amidst intense fighting, she was fatally wounded in the head and died in her cockpit. Her airplane continued to fly itself, steady and level, heading northwest for more than 200 kilometers until it finally ran out of fuel and crashed. When her body was recovered, she was still wearing under her flight suit, the brassiere made of parachute silk with the distinctive red stripe. Antonia's airplane was excavated and her body taken to a mass grave.

Learning of the discovery of Antonina, with Lilia's title still unresolved, Ina and her husband hatched a new plan. In 1985 Ina and her husband had located Antonina Lebedeva's body in a mass grave and arranged to borrow it. They would deliver to the Soviet government an elaborate story about the day they had found Lilia's body. It was a story about a boy on a motorcycle who had been searching with them that day, and chased a snake down a hole. In the hole he discovered a piece of an airplane wing. Under the wing was the body of Lilia Litvyak, still wearing a brassiere made of parachute silk with a distinctive red stripe that Ina had made for her as proof that it was indeed the body of Lilia Litvyak. Along with the story, they delivered for official examination, the body of Antonina Lebedeva. They were the same height, and they wore the same uniform. Soviet officials could find no discrepancies. It was determined that Lilia had been killed in battle from a fatal head wound on the 1st of August, 1943. The official record of her service was changed from 'missing in action' to 'killed in action,' making Lilia eligible for the nation's highest honor. Another petition was filed, detailing her service record and accomplishments in the war, with the request to the Soviet state that Lilia be given the title of Hero. Once again, the request was denied.

While the problems caused by socialist central planning and one-size-fits-all solutions piled up faster than the freshest gobbledygook of Marxist ideology could explain them away, Lilia's story and her legend refused to abate. The Soviet state appeared ever more as a monolith of bureaucracy that disdained the individual and cared nothing at all for the human soul. With no way to admit or reconcile its own failures, it existed only to perpetuate itself. In 1991, after seventy years of failed policies, the U.S.S.R. (The Union of Soviet Socialist Republics) was dissolved, and the Communist Party itself was outlawed as a criminal gang. It would come to be known as the "Soviet Mistake." But a year before this occurred, in 1990, something gave way. The hard line of Communism had begun to crack. Lilia Litvyak would be granted her title, and Yuri Litvyak, then 60 years old, would hold in his hand Lilia's gold star.

Lilia Litvyak was a paradox that had come full circle. For the crime of being her father's daughter she was classified a traitor. By her deeds in the war, to the people she was a hero. For being captured she was classified a traitor once more. In May of 1990, by the pen of Premier Gorbachev, her picture on the front page of the national newspaper, *Pravda*, Lilia Litvyak was finally and officially declared a Hero of the Soviet Union.

EPILOGUE

I might have called this Chapter 16, but it was never my intention to become any part of this story myself. It was in March of 1999 that I travelled to Moscow, in post-Soviet Russia, to follow up and fact check a story I thought might have the elements for a good movie; action, adventure, a love story. I conducted a series of interviews, with the then current Colonel of the 73rd Guards Regiment, and a previous Colonel of the 73rd Guards who had become something of a regimental historian. I also met Lilia's mechanic, Ina Pasportnikova, and a chief mechanic from the 586th fighter regiment who had also been Katya Budanova's mechanic for a time. I met a journalist from Pravda who had written stories about Lilia, doing his own part to keep her story alive, as well as several female veteran pilots of the 588th known as the "Nightwitches." In these interviews, I was told conflicting accounts. What was the true fate of Lilia Litvyak, the world's first female ace fighter pilot? It was soon apparent to me that I had stumbled into a mystery. There today stands the monument in the Donbass, in the town of Krasnyi-Luch, a posthumously awarded Gold Star for Hero of the Soviet Union, and a story about her body being found after a decades long search. Yet the stories didn't match. Two Colonels from the 73rd Guards, one present and one previous, each told different tales of how the war had ended for Lieutenant Litvyak. I interviewed the two female mechanics, and again was told two different tales.

As I first read the account of Ina finding Lilia's body, before my trip to Moscow, the details seemed oddly arranged. There was the fatal head wound and the red-striped brassiere. But it was the detail of a boy on a motorcycle chasing a snake down a hole that stood out. It struck me as precisely the kind of colorful detail one would add to a fake story or a staged event to make it appear unimpeachably true. It seemed to me then to be a clumsy detail included as part of a script.

I met Ina and her husband in their apartment outside of Moscow. Ina was then seventy-nine years old. Although their barren cupboards displayed the bleakness of the post-Soviet economy at the time, they seemed happy, approaching what some have called the second childhood. When I asked Ina about the day she had found Lilia's body, she scratched her head and seemed confused, as though she had no recollection at all of any such thing having occurred. In that awkward moment, her husband nudged her with his elbow and smiled as if to say: *"Hey, remember the script."*

Ina's face lit up suddenly as she remembered it. "Oh, yes!" Ina proclaimed, thrusting a finger in the air. "There was a boy on a motorcycle!" she said, then loyally retold the tale.

I later met the chief mechanic of the 586th fighter regiment, and the pieces of the story further fell into place. After an annual meeting of surviving members of the female flying regiments in Moscow, I was invited to her Moscow apartment and was served beet soup. She had compiled war records of her own, scouring declassified archives, seeking the true history that had been hidden in Soviet times.

"If Ina had never been searching for Lilia, then who?" I asked.

It has been said that Russian history is extremely unpredictable. I also found this to be true. While I do not know the details of her fate after the 1st of August, 1943, I do believe Lilia Litvyak survived the war. In the year 2000, a year after my visit to Moscow, an old Russian woman appeared on Swiss television describing herself in a televised interview as a former combat pilot. Was it Lilia Litvyak, finally free enough to reveal herself some fifty-seven years after disappearing over the front? It was said that some pilots of the 586th fighter regiment believed as much. If rumors are true, Lilia chose not to return to the Soviet Union at war's end. Instead she escaped to politically neutral Switzerland where she married and had three children, passing the decades in an otherwise anonymous life. So it ends with a mystery, Dear Reader. I cannot give you a final, definitive ending. This is merely a story about a story, and the people who would tell it.

—*Christopher P. Redwine, 2021*